WHERE ARE WE NOW?

WHERE ARE WE NOW?

GLENN PATTERSON

An Apollo Book

9 7 5 3 1 2 4 6 8

A catalogue record for this book is available from
the British Library.

ISBN (HB): 9781838931988
ISBN (XTPB): 9781838931995
ISBN (E): 9781838932015

Typeset by Divaddict Publishing Solutions Ltd

Printed and bound in Great Britain by
CPI Group (UK) Ltd, Croydon CRO 4YY

Head of Zeus Ltd
First Floor East
5–8 Hardwick Street
London EC1R 4RG

WWW.HEADOFZEUS.COM

To you, who picked it up, to borrow or to buy.
Thank you.

1

Somebody had stolen his identity. An elaborate, thorough-going fraud stretching back years – decades. The evidence had all been laid out on the table before him, staggering in its scope and audacity: passports in two nationalities, staff cards, union cards, mortgage agreements, loan applications, a marriage certificate, flawlessly executed, photographs – lots and lots of photographs, starting on the steps of the wedding church, with their sprinkling of confetti, running on then through reception and honeymoon (Paris by the looks of it), to holidays by the sea, Christmas trees, works' dinners, charity discos, fun runs, hill walks, at least *five* identically posed with this character leaning his arm on the roofs of new cars – Fiesta, Allegro, Renault 12, 21, Citroën C5 – the receipts for which were in a separate envelope in a different box, along with the cooker receipts, the fridge receipts, the serial television and television recording device receipts, Betamax to Blu-ray... it would have taken a lifetime near to go through it in detail, and at the end of it all, he told his doctor (for despite all that evidence he had a hunch this was still more a medical than a legal matter), he would still have looked up and said, hand on heart, I have no idea who this person is, but it's not me.

The doctor leaned back in her seat, fingers laced on her stomach. She was on the home straight now to retirement. She had wisdom to dispense.

'Don't take this the wrong way,' she said, 'but half the people in this country probably wish they had your problem.' On the wall to her left was a sketch of the half-timbered 1920s surgery that had been extended and adapted with ever decreasing sympathy from the 1940s on until finally in the early 2000s it was demolished altogether and they built the current health centre, containing the wall and the sketch and the doctor leaning back in her seat addressing Herbie. 'Anyway, look around you,' she gestured towards the window – skyline of cranes and cloud-reflecting glass – though her scope was greater by far, 'the whole world is unlike itself. Lord help us, you hardly know when you go to bed whether you are going to wake up in the same country.'

'That's maybe not the comfort that you think it is.'

'Try this, then: you're here, aren't you?'

'You mean breathing-in-and-out here?'

'I mean sitting-in-this-room here.' She turned the computer screen so that Herbie could see it. 'All that?' A column of densely packed sentences. She clicked and another column appeared below it, or the same column grew another foot in length. 'That's you, from the moment your mother heave-hoed you into the loving arms of the NHS. And this' – she typed – Herbie read the day's date and further on a phrase that might have included 'mild dissociation' – 'this is you too: same story, new instalment.'

She stopped. 'If I said Toome to you – capital T, double-o, em, ee – what's the first word comes into your head?'

'Bridge.'

'OK, the second.'

'Bypass.'

'Exactly. You sort of know the place is there still, but I bet you if I was to plonk you down in the middle of it again you wouldn't recognise a bit of it.'

He kneaded his temples with thumb and ring finger. Some days it felt as though he was carrying a concrete block around in there, some days an empty box. 'Do you think I need a prescription?'

'Yes: don't sit up late at night looking at old photos.'

He thought as he left it might finally be time he changed doctors. Dr Ross had come with Tanya as part of the marriage package. 'I've been with her since I was seven. She got me through puberty practically single-handed.' Tanya's mother had lived in complete denial of anything below the collarbone, hers or her daughter's. 'I wouldn't go to anyone else.' It had been all right while he still had a car, but for the past few years now he had been taking two buses across town for appointments, two buses back. You would want to set aside a morning, or like today an afternoon.

He got on the first of the return buses a short distance from the health centre and got off again among the cranes and the cloud-reflecting glass, just short of the City Hall – the clock

3

on the old Robinson and Cleaver building, facing, read twenty to three – and before he had gone ten yards had had a leaflet pressed into his hand.

'City sightseeing tours,' said the presser, a tall youth in a red all-weather jacket, 'hop on, hop off.'

Ten yards further on an older man in a blue jacket handed him another leaflet, 'See the city, one-day, two-day tickets.'

Now that he looked in fact there were red and blue jackets whichever way he turned, importuning passersby from the same crossings and corners where once upon a not so very long ago evening-newspaper sellers guldered – *Sixth… Late… Tele-o!*

Where had they all gone?

Was that them – some of them – in the red and blue jackets? They had the same deftness of movement, the little jinks now to this side now to that, the ability to catch an eye, pick out one hand among the many before it could be snatched away.

He tried to think when he had last bought a newspaper on the street. Ceasefire maybe. IT'S OVER! Who hadn't bought that one?

Who then had ever seen or even dreamed of Belfast tour buses?

A large party of elderly people – American, he was going to say – one or two in precautionary rain macs (for even at twenty to three the day had yet to declare its hand), Titanic Experience bags hanging from their right wrists, wandered past Queen Victoria, a study in rising coldly above, and out of the City Hall grounds and from all sides the red and blue jackets converged.

New cruise ship in town. Two thousand more souls in search of diversion. A better than even chance Herbie would be seeing some of them before the week was out.

But not today. There was a bus about to pull out, common or garden Translink variety. Herbie got on it (it was a kneeling bus: no need thankfully to hop)… got off – easy does it – twenty eastward-tending minutes later, on the far side of the Lagan, at the stop next to the Christians All Together Church – aka the CATCH, motto, 'The catch? There is no catch, only the ever-open arms of Jesus.' There was a gesture went with it, a salute almost: arms crossed, palms spread against the breast, then thrust – Radio goo-goo, radio ga-ga – into the air.

The church had started life in a wooden meeting hall on the site of a newsagent's that caught the force of a bomb meant for a government office. It was still a corner shop of a place when Herbie first encountered it, but had grown so exponentially since that it was verging now on megastore, with its crèche and state-of-the-art young people's centre and even, he had been told, its own in-house solicitors, insurance brokers, estate agents and financial advisers.

He sometimes had the sense – he had it again now – as he was walking away from the bus stop that the church was actually creeping up the road behind him on brickie-toes. *Quick, quick* – shoulders hunched – *duck in the door of this cafe…* Sam's.

Cue sub-Bacharachian soundtrack. Now That's What I Call Knock-off.

Derek, Sam's partner, was at the counter on his own, hands

splayed either side of an iPad, eyebrows gathered into a frown. A hand-painted sign above the archway to his right, leading to what the previous owners had tried to style the Terrace, read 'Outdoor Debating and Tobacco Appreciation Society. <u>Views</u>' (the underline was unsteady) '<u>May Be Aired</u>'.

'Cheeky bastards,' Derek said to the iPad. To Herbie, rotating the device 180 degrees, 'Did you see this?'

The iPad was open, as if to prove a point about these newspaperless times, at the local BBC website. Herbie's brain did a double take.

'Is that a...'

'Yep.'

'You're not serious?'

Someone had dumped a Portakabin on one of the roads running up to the hills on the far west of the city.

'That's just nuts.'

It looked from the picture as though all the valuable, resalable stuff had been stripped out, the metal, the plumbing, the cladding, so it was barely hanging together, but still...

'A *Portakabin*.' Derek spun the iPad round to face himself again. 'I mean I can understand a bed or a three-piece suite or a whole load of scrap metal.' The Belfast hills had long been the go-to place for the city's fly-tippers. And not just this city's. Bags of clinical waste had been found up there that could be traced back to hospitals in Limerick. 'But, like, think about it. First of all you would need a thing bigger than a Portakabin to carry it, a trailer, or one of those low-loaders. What... twenty-five feet long? Thirty?'

'Thirty, easy, I'd say,' Herbie did say: the sort of thing they would close off a lane of motorway for if you were doing it legitimately.

'Right, and you would need a team of men as well or a heavy-duty hoist.'

'Or both.'

'Exactly.' He was getting into his stride now, Derek. (He was built around a nose, and when he talked his head seemed pulled this way and that by it.) 'You would need time, too, a fair bit of time and, like, even then you'd have to be pretty confident no one was going to come along and catch you at it. There'd have to be other people in the know, scouts. There'd have to be a whole chain of knowing and not really giving two fucks. That's what it comes down to. Am I right? From the person who hands over the five hundred quid or whatever less than he thought he was going to have to pay to have the thing taken care of, to the people who were slipped a few pound to look the other way, to whoever it was drove off and left that thing sitting there on the side of the Upper Springfield Road: not really giving two fucks... That's lovely.' These last two words to the woman with the buggy (and child that really shouldn't be in it at all at his age) who had set a saucer on the counter with her bill and a five-pound note.

'Hold on, your change.'

'Put it in the jar.'

Herbie got the door. (The child in the buggy stuck out his tongue and quickly covered up his mouth with his hand.)

Derek did as bid – 'Thank you!' – with the change. Picked up where he had left off. 'Know what I think? Instead of the council losing out twice over – I mean, the dumping fees are gone already and now they're going to have to salvage it, whatever that's going to set them back – they could just let it sit there – a big Portakabin-y monument. To Two Fucks Not Given.'

'They could maybe set a few diesel cubes alongside.'

'Diesel whats?'

'Cubes. When they launder the diesel...' It had always seemed to Herbie such an inappropriate word: launder. Sulphuric acid he thought he remembered hearing they used to remove the green dye that identified the fuel as intended only for farm machinery down South. '... The waste from it, they put it into these giant plastic cubes. Did you never see them?' He opened his arms to their full extent to give a sense of the dimensions. 'The really environmentally conscious launderers bury them in a hole in the middle of somebody's field. The others...'

'The Ungivers of Fuck.'

'Twice over... them, they just turf it off the back of their vans wherever they feel like it, laneways, verges, rivers...'

Herbie had always associated the trade with the Peacetime IRA. What they didn't launder themselves they taxed the freelancers on. There was a kind of logic to it – you draw an arbitrary line across our island, we'll profit by smuggling diesel and anything else that can be lifted and moved backwards and forwards over it. And if we poison the water supply while we're about it, well whose fault's that? *The longer you stay here, the sicker everybody'll get.*

Derek spread his fingers till the Portakabin's blurred bare bones filled the screen. 'Here's what I love about the Portakabin. This councillor has come out and said Belfast is not a dumping ground for people trying to get round paying for disposing of things the right way. Can you believe that? It *is* a dumping ground, you… you *balloon*, you' – as though the councillor and not the words attributed to him were right in front of him – 'that's why the bloody thing is sitting there, that's why all the other shit is there.'

He stopped, turned to the espresso machine. 'Coffee?'

'Just a small one.'

'Go sit, I'll bring it.'

The cafe at this time of the day was sparsely populated. (It was never exactly what you would call heaving.) Herbie made his way past a woman playing Sudoku on her phone and a man sitting between two nursery-school-age children, like the referee in a colouring-in competition, and pulled out a chair at his preferred table by the window underneath the capital S of Sam's. The table itself was I, all the tables being identified by giant Scrabble letters rather than by numbers, starting arbitrarily at B and stopping at S, with no sign anywhere of L, M, N, O or P. You might have expected tile racks for menu holders, but like much else in Sam's you got the feeling it hadn't been fully thought through. Neither that nor the fact that most of what they had furnished their cafe with came from other cafes that had already failed.

Derek in particular saw things, liked them, bought them and then wondered afterwards where they might go. How they might.

Someone had swapped around the table letters so that Herbie's table was flanked on one side by D and on the other by C and K.

Derek set the coffee down on the table. 'I'll leave you to your devotions,' he said and lifted D and C to return them to their rightful places.

Herbie was pretty much down to one cup of coffee a day now. The less he drank, the more ritual attached to it. It was something of a motif in his life, contraction to the point of concentration. He placed his hands flat on the table, spread his fingers until his thumbs were almost – almost – not... quite... touching. A long breath out. Now. As he raised the cup to his lips, Peadar passed on the far side of the street in his familiar forward-tilting gait, Norrie bouncing along a couple of heartbeats behind.

Herbie set his cup down. You couldn't drink coffee and watch Norrie.

Norrie wasn't the only three-legged dog Herbie had ever met, but he was the only one he had met that was born that way. Peadar said he would bet on him any day of the week up against a dog with four. Faster in the pee-stops for a start: nothing to lift. 'Give him another leg now he wouldn't know what to do with it.'

First time they met, Peadar had introduced him to Herbie as a rescue dog. 'What do you know?' said Herbie. 'I suppose

I always thought of them as bigger, you know, brandy barrels and everything.'

'He doesn't *do* rescues. It was me rescued him, or the kennels I picked him up from did.'

'I am a complete dope,' Herbie said, to which Peadar had replied that his father had schooled him to believe that even a wise man could say a foolish thing, but that, yes, Herbie was a bit of a dope all right.

Even so, Herbie had never been able to shake the thought entirely: Peadar sitting in an armchair of an evening, Norrie stretched out on the rug in front of the fire, head on his paws, then a phone beeping – a special tone – incoming message, the dog's left ear pricking up. Peadar sitting forward then, putting on his reading glasses, scrolling down the text for his mission, on his feet, Norrie with him – *No time to lose!*

At the door of the Post Office, Peadar bent to whisper in the dog's ear before stepping inside. Norrie angled his tail, folded his back leg neatly on the ground and sat, beneath the wedge-shaped To Let sign, whose sudden appearance the year before, or the speculation that it triggered – Jamie Oliver in two words – was the reason why Sam's was Sam's and not, as it had been since long before Herbie moved to that side of town, The Tea Caddy.

'Couldn't sign the deeds over fast enough,' Sam told him on the day they opened. 'I thought they were going to kiss my hand.'

'I thought they were going to go further than that,' said Derek.

Neeta, who had been with the Post Office from the year dot, and had from dot and a day taken all her tea breaks in the Caddy, had been the one to let the JO kitten (well, even at forty-something, she could never think of him as a full-grown cat) out of the bag. Fifteen months on and not a sniff of a new tenant, she was mortified. 'To think I might have scared those poor people away,' she said, even though if pushed (and not all that hard) she would have said, yes, she much preferred the cafe as it was under Sam and Derek. And, no, she didn't suppose the Caddy's owners, sitting on the deck of the house they had bought in Marbella on the proceeds of the sale, very much missed getting up in the dark on winter mornings or carting waste out to the giant bins in the back alley at the end of every day.

From Neeta too had come the news that specially trained staff were to be brought in two mornings a week ahead of the closure to help familiarise senior citizens with online banking and benefits payments, although the commencement date for that had also been revised back several times in the past year and a bit.

The senior citizens Herbie had overheard in the cafe discussing the closure were split between those (OK, *that*: there were only two of them) already mourning the passing of the Post Office – the yarns you would have in queues in the good old days – and those/that saying there was nothing good about the old days at all. 'I mind once standing a full hour to draw a tenner. I tell you, I did a jig when they put the first cash machine in outside.'

What nobody had yet told Neeta – under her breath this, though there happened to be only Herbie and Derek in the cafe at that precise moment, and with a glance first over her shoulder – was who was going to counsel the guys who came in every Monday morning with the carrier bags of cash for deposit. She had mouthed to Herbie and Derek the three initials familiar from a score of paramilitary murals within ten minutes' walk of Sam's front door.

Derek said, 'They don't really?'

'They do. Really.'

'Bags of actual cash? That all sounds a bit 1970s. I mean, I thought there were laws now.'

'There are, and they can give you chapter and verse themselves... unusual payments, which theirs aren't since they're there every week; no more than nine thousand pounds, which theirs never are, even if that means there's two or three of them in succession coming up to your window. They even offer advice on filling in Suspicious Activity Reports for the Financial Intelligence Unit, knowing fine well that having any sort of a conversation with them about a report would be an offence under the Proceeds of Crime Act. We're standing there counting their money and they are literally laughing in our faces.'

'What do you reckon to that?' Derek asked when Neeta was gone.

'I don't think she'd make it up.'

'Imagine something was to happen,' Derek said. 'Between the front door and the counter, say. Say one of their bags was to go missing somehow… That would be the test, wouldn't it? Who would they report it to? The police?'

Herbie had shrugged. 'I don't know, but if I was the person who had made one of their bags go missing, I think I would be taking it straight round to my undertaker, save any delays: give me the finest coffin a couple of pence under nine thousand pounds can buy.'

Peadar appeared again now at the Post Office door. Norrie jumped to and got a chuck under the chin for his patience. On they went together, full tilt and partial list.

Herbie turned his attention again to his coffee. A little bit of time got away from him while he drank, with no clear thoughts to account for it. And sometimes that was all right.

He needed a couple of bits and pieces of shopping so decided to take the scenic route home, by M&S Simply Food (it had been a better sentence when it was still Iceland, easier on the pocket too), stopping at the door to pick up a basket in which was abandoned a leaflet for a pet crematorium. Calculations in the margin for something smaller than the headline cat and dog figures… actually, for two things. Tortoises? Guinea pigs? Tragic accident? Pact? He couldn't bring himself to bin it but handed it instead, as he came back round towards the tills, to the security guard. (Herbie had long ago given up trying to predict when she would be there, which days were deemed least secure.) 'Somebody's heart must be broken,' the guard said and carried the leaflet respectfully across her open palms to her station in the corner of the store.

Brian was on the ten items or less till. Herbie would have lined up behind the bulkier buyers, gone back round even and picked up a couple more things he didn't actually need to put himself over the limit, only Brian, following the movement of the security guard, caught his eye. 'Come here and I'll take you.'

Heavy was his heart as he set his basket down.

'No work today?' Brian asked.

'Doctor's.'

'Ah!'

He started ringing in the items, frowning, which was a giveaway.

'Man walks in here earlier the day,' he said, 'looking for a pair of stockings for his wife.'

'Is this a joke?'

'Says she has been going on and on about this kind she saw on the shopping channel, never stretch, never ladder, never even smell.'

'It is a joke.'

Brian had his hand out. Herbie put a twenty in it.

'Here's me, stockings that never stretch, never ladder, never even smell...? That's nylon impossible.' He allowed the line to sit then gave it an extra little nudge. 'Ny-lon... Nigh on...?'

Herbie had long ago exhausted his lifetime's reserve of polite laughter on Brian's jokes.

'That actually hurt.'

Brian smiled. If you couldn't get a laugh get a wince. 'Twelve pounds twenty-one change… See you again soon.'

'In the nicest possible way, Brian,' Herbie said, 'I really hope not.'

There were a few spits and spots of rain as he exited the automatic doors. He thought of the American tourists in their macs. *Didn't we tell ya it always rained? Didn't we tell ya?* By the time he had got to his own corner, though, it had stopped again. He paused a moment, swapping his bag from left hand to right. The street looked, with an hour to go yet before the great end-of-day parking scramble began, as the developers a hundred and some years ago must have imagined it would always look, not a car in sight: two long opposing terraces, each interrupted halfway down by an entry leading on to an alleyway, which some residents treated as an extension of their backyards, with barbecues going in summer, fairy lights in winter, and some – having no mountain within easy reach and not giving that much of a fuck who picked up after them – treated as the repository for all that they had grown beyond or had failed them, the id to the ego of their neat front rooms.

Herbie felt an upsurge of affection at the sight of it. To begin with, it was true, he had had to fight the thought of the place where he lived as a settlement, rather than a home, that portion left to him after the division of the marital estate, or semi- in his and Tanya's case. ('Oriel', their old house had been called. A long-lost kingdom, which might have been asking for it.) In fact, it had the comforting sense of the familiar: he had grown up in a house just like it… his entire life in between

16

now seeming like one of those Escher staircase engravings – up and up and up to arrive at the place from which he had started.

There were, he had discovered within days of moving in, settlements to the immediate left of him and two doors to the right, and an unsettlement facing, proceedings in that case being then still pending. The woman who lived there kept her blinds permanently tilted, as though refusing to acknowledge even to herself that she was there, that this thing was happening to *her*, Audrey Bannon. She scowled at neighbours she bumped into on the street, despite her best attempts at avoidance, like it was their fault, all of it, right back to her husband stumbling in at two in the morning that time with the dirty neck he seriously tried to tell her came from catching the strap of his shoulder bag in the taxi door, for that, again despite her best attempts, was the story that had got out. That and the fact that he had ended up in a heap at the bottom of the stairs (he was far too pissed to have broken anything vital), which was why she was the one to move out, complete with restraining order, pending those proceedings, and he stayed put.

And here's the thing – Herbie thought it again now as he reached his front gate and glanced, instinctively, across at those blinds, yes, still tilted to repel, several years and one lost court case on – he wasn't so sure she was wrong. *Hang on for as long as you can, because once you let go there's no calling back the true feeling of any of it.*

Tanya emailed him a couple of times a month, chatty letters of the kind he remembered her writing to old school friends, all past intimacy between the two of them now on a par with them having once been assigned adjacent lockers. She sent him photographs too sometimes, the beach holidays she had not wanted to go on when she was with him (it was her objected to them, wasn't it?): this is good of Martin, not so good of me (it was the other way round of course). Very occasionally there would be a line or two delivered as it were out the corner of her mouth, or behind the locker door: *God Bless HRT…! Can you imagine if there'd been Tinder when we were young? The fortune we'd have saved on drink… They've found a polyp on the lining of my womb, completely benign, I am happy to say and – even happier (as is Martin!) – not having any other* (double underline) *adverse effects.*

Herbie closed the door behind him.

Home.

A mismatched pair of shoeboxes was still sitting out on the table at the dining end of the knock-through. Dining, computing, sitting some weekends with the Sunday papers from one end of the day to the other. He swept up the alien-seeming passports, the union cards, the car and TV receipts, *the evidence*, scattered round about, and pressed them down on top, then lifted the boxes one after the other and set them with two others at the foot of the table. He eyed them balefully all the way through dinner then the moment he was finished took the whole lot up to the spare room and shut the door.

The doctor was probably right.

He needed something else to do with his nights.

His days too, possibly.

2

His days had for the best part of three decades been filled with other people's pay packets: uneventfully, those people would probably say, which was fair enough. It was one of those jobs – what was the saying? 'For those who know, no explanation is necessary; for those who don't, no explanation is possible.' If no one beyond the Wages Department door was aware of the dramas involved in getting out three hundred and fifty pay packets from month to month then he and all those who worked with and eventually under him were doing their job.

You'd be standing in the canteen, and a couple of guys would join the queue. 'Herbie. Anything strange or startling?' And you'd think, should I actually? But, no, 'Not a thing,' you'd say.

Ah, who was he kidding, it *was* uneventful.

Then the Crash came.

Almost overnight the three hundred and fifty pay packets – or their (by then) electronic equivalents – shrank by a hundred, then fifty more and carried on shrinking, in the couple of years that followed, by twenties and tens before settling at eighty. The Wages Department shrank from seven to five to two. Then even two became too expensive to maintain. It was staring him in the face every month, as was the solution: outsourcing, in a word.

And, of course, if it was staring him in the face it had to be staring other people, higher up, too. It mightn't have come as a complete surprise, but the end was still a shock, though nothing like the shock of what came after. What didn't.

Nobody was hiring, or nobody who was was hiring anybody like him.

For the first few months he felt utterly becalmed.

Then one morning he got a letter from New Zealand – a cousin he had last (and first) met in the early seventies at their grandparents' diamond wedding anniversary dinner and had corresponded with maybe four or five times in all the years since. (Her letter had been forwarded from Oriel and included best wishes to Tanya.) She hoped he didn't mind her writing to him like this, but her husband was coming on fifty in a few months and she wanted to surprise him with his family tree, which like her own had roots 'over there'. Only problem was she hadn't a clue how to go about it: the websites she had been on up to now sent her round in circles. Herbie hadn't much more of a clue, beyond knowing how to find his way to the Records Office, but he did have, as never before in his life, time on his hands – lots and lots of time – and over the next few weeks he was able to uncover just enough to persuade himself that he maybe wasn't completely useless after all and

– of far greater importance to his cousin – exactly the right amount to fit the genuine Connemara bog oak frame that she had already had made to display the family tree in. A friend of his cousin who was at the house the night of the fiftieth birthday – the grand unveiling – then got in touch asking him for help and put the fruits of his research up on Facebook, along with her undying gratitude, after which the requests started coming in from everywhere.

Still, he had been at it more than a year before he felt able to refer to himself as a freelance researcher or had the confidence to deal with queries from people who had simply fetched up at the Records Office on spec, days when he was there. Their numbers had been steadily climbing, the other researchers told him, but in the past couple of years they had rocketed. He was in there two or three days a week now out of season, all the hours God sent, if he'd been willing to accept them, April to October, when the cruise ships were in town, guiding searchers through the idiosyncrasies of local spelling and pronunciation and the occasionally haphazard transcription of early-nineteenth-century church clerks.

On one of his first visits to the Records Office he had run into another freelancer – actually would have had to take extreme steps to avoid him. The man – Sean Copeland you called him – stood, as though it was his official station, just inside the door of the reading room, keeping an eye out over the shoulder of whoever he happened to be in conversation with in case anyone lost-looking wandered in. It was hard to put an exact age on him – closer to seventy than sixty, certainly. He had used to manage a bar just north of the city centre – had worked in the trade since he left school – and then one Friday lunchtime in 1975 two fellas with flour sacks over their heads walked in and sprayed the place with bullets, killing four of his regulars and a trainee barman who had only started the afternoon before. Sean had booked himself out that lunchtime to go and see the dentist – lost a filling eating a Toffo he'd found in his pocket – so was spared: spared too having to see the very worst of the aftermath, though what he saw, when he arrived a quarter of an hour after the last ambulance left, was bad enough. He helped with the clear-up, went to all five of the funerals, saw that the bar was got ready for reopening, then walked away. 'Just hadn't the heart for it any more. Haven't so much as crossed the door of a pub since.'

It made sense of his stance, though, there inside the door of the Records Office reading room. That was his bar now. The chat probably wasn't that much different. *Do you not mind him? Big tall fella? His wife's sister married a man whose grandmother on his mother's side was one of the Suffragettes who dug up the greens at Fortwilliam Golf Club with kitchen forks.*

It was Sean who introduced Herbie to tithes, or to be absolutely accurate, Church of Ireland tithe applotments, 1823–37, a particularly narrow area of expertise, as he cheerfully admitted, but many indeed were the furrows in history where ancestors might lie hidden: the trenches, rather.

This, Sean explained, was deep-sea diving, the abyssal zone, compared to snorkelling in the shallows of births, deaths and marriages. The records had been rendered in negative, inky black cells flooding the screen of the microfiche reader (itself in this slimline world of laptops and tablets as ungainly as a manatee) and teeming with strange luminescent squiggles that on first encounter bore little relation to actual handwriting. At the very, very bottom, where some parish clerk had tried to make sure he didn't go over a page, there was barely a peak or a tail to hold on to and the squiggles aspired to the condition of flat line.

'Just think,' said Sean, 'this might be the only trace this human being left. All those decades of living, all those dreams and disappointments, reduced to this. It's got to be worth the effort to coax it up to the surface.'

Sean kept all his research notes in these little red notebooks that you could pick up for less than a pound in any filling station or newsagent's, preferred sending letters (written in ballpoint pen) rather than emails to clients, and always made duplicates. (Carbon paper, not photocopy.)

When, a couple of years after Herbie met him, Sean died – in his sleep, lying on his back the way he always lay, his wife, Hannah, said, as though all these years he had been in training – Herbie went round to the house to pay his respects.

Hannah had taken Herbie through the kitchen and out to the shed – it more or less filled the small back garden – that had been her husband's study, where there were scores of red notebooks bound together with elastic bands, dates on the front of the ones on top going back to 1975, six weeks after the shooting in the bar, boxes of his duplicate letters and the letters they were replying to. 'What on earth am I going to do with them all?' she asked. Three of the yellow-and-black pencils he always used lay on the little card table, freshly sharpened, perfectly aligned. She picked one of them up, pressed the point against her finger until she grimaced. 'Don't think me heartless, but I'm not sure I could bear to have to look at it all.'

Later he thought he should have suggested straight away that she donate it to the Records Office. But, no, 'I'll look after it, if you want,' was what he said.

'Oh, I wouldn't want to be putting you to a whole lot of trouble.'

'You wouldn't be, it wouldn't be.'

They filled her Fiat Uno, back seat and footwells as well as boot, and still had to go back for more.

'Are you sure you have the room for it?' Hannah asked when they pulled up outside Herbie's front gate the first time.

'There's only me there,' he said, and instantly wished he hadn't. As if she needed reminding she was on her own now too.

They stood together at last in the empty shed. 'What do you think you will use it for now?'

'Honestly? I think I'll knock it down. It's been blocking the sun at the back of the house from the day and hour it went up.'

Last time Herbie visited there was decking with a rattan corner sofa, grandchildren's toys scattered everywhere.

The notebooks meanwhile remained untouched in their boxes in Herbie's spare room. If he was being honest with himself, he was daunted by the responsibility. Those many, many years of painstaking research in his hands.

He would get round to collating and cataloguing it all.

Soon.

A few months back, he had taken on a little bit of extra work filing in the Records Office archive – 0.2 of a Grade F, seven and a half hours a week. Hardly a fortune, but it kept him ticking over and gave him access besides to staff services and perks.

The Records Office was a half hour's walk from the house, a couple of minutes longer coming back, the penultimate stretch being uphill almost as far as Sam's, where the road levelled out just long enough for him to think as he put the key in his front door – two streets further along on the right – he would be fine doing this tomorrow again after all.

The route to work took him through an area known as the Rivers – Mersey Street, Severn Street, Tamar Street, Frome, Derwent, Tern – and over the Dee Street Bridge and into the old harbour estate – the shipyard – for ten ship-free years now the Titanic Quarter. At the Dee Street end of the bridge was a hoarding, 'You Must Be Born Again'. At the far end, just beyond the roundabout that routed all but a trickle of outbound traffic away from Dee Street itself and on to the Sydenham Bypass (Bangor that direction, M1, M2 and M3 the other), a new Porsche dealership was nearing completion, a hundred yards from the BMW one – a great hangar of a place that, any time Herbie passed it, was as busy as a Bank Holiday ferry port.

As he crested the bridge the morning after his doctor's appointment, two feet where in industrial boom-times gone by there were thousands from the Rivers below, the sun put in an appearance. For a few moments while his eyes adjusted, every window in the city seemed to sparkle. Cars on the Sydenham Bypass to his left were daytime shooting stars. He slipped off his jacket and folded it over his arm. Take your summer while you can get it, the Belfast watchword.

The pedestrian traffic got heavier as he carried on along the Sydenham Road – the tail end of the morning commute coming out of the footpath down from Titanic Halt, bound for the Metropolitan College and the tech and finance companies further down towards the end of what his father used to call the East Twin Island.

His father had worked there straight out of his apprenticeship, already saving up to get married, when – 'sorry, lad, but you know the drill, last in first out' – he got given his cards: a Thursday, just before the dinner hour. Him and his mate, who'd been second last in, heard they were starting men in a factory in one of the new industrial estates out in the eastern suburbs, so they walked with their toolboxes to the train station on the edge of the harbour estate (apartments now) and put them in left luggage then jumped on a bus, which was packed with men who had heard the same thing they had – had to go all the way to the top for a seat – and of course when they arrived at the factory everyone else got up to get off ahead of them. (Last on... last out.) By the time they reached the factory the foreman was taking the 'Men Wanted' sign down off the gate. He said to them, but, they might be starting more men in a couple of weeks if they wanted to leave their names, so that's what they did then caught the bus back down to the station, and here, when they got on, didn't they get talking to a fella who had worked in the shipyard with them and who told them there was a wee shop specialising in panel welding, a couple of stops short of the station, and *he* had it from another fella that they were starting men in there. So when the bus pulled in again and your man was getting off they got off with him, and he was right: they were starting men, and it was a *wee* shop. 'You'd have bigger sitting rooms nowadays. Cobbles on the floor – inside, I mean – and the only light from a skylight that was wiped once a week with a cloth on a broom handle, though all that did was move the dirt around, spread the gloom a bit.'

Two questions, the interview consisted of: do you have your union cards – good – and do you have your own tools? 'We were just on our way to get them.'

'Well go yous on and get them and I'll start you as soon as you are back.'

And that was them, started. They had been out of work for two and a half hours.

'Gentleman of the reformed faith, was he, your father?' asked a colleague in Wages to whom Herbie had once told this story, the colleague's point being that jobs in those industries, even in wee shops with cobbles and filthy skylights ('I was never as glad to get out of a place in my life,' his dad's story ended) tended in those pre-Troubles years to be the preserve of Protestants.

'He was, but his mate wasn't.'

'The exception that proves the rule then.'

His dad's mate had moved to America at the start of the Seventies, worried about his son getting sucked in. (Herbie's dad's term? Herbie's dad's mate's?) Herbie wondered if this was the boy whose bedroom he had sat in once, while the adults talked downstairs, pitching their voices low (the very definition of Troubled), a creased *Club International* that had already passed through – paused in – many hands open on his lap. Was *he* even the other boy? Whose heart shrank hearing the word 'minge' for the first time? Whose thoughts were haunted by it long, long after the pictures that had caused it to be uttered had dimmed in his mind's eye.

Maybe that wasn't the day then when he sat in the family car, trying to ignore the fact that his dad was sitting, separated from him by more than just the gap between the seats, crying through fingertips pressed to his eyes. 'Best workmate I ever had. Best workmate anybody ever had.'

'I couldn't stand being in the same room as him,' a woman said, to the little white stubs coming out of her ears Herbie assumed, since no one around her, and him, at the pedestrian crossing he had reached responded, although everyone else, apart from Herbie, was absorbed in their own hand-held or wrist-worn devices, checking steps, heartbeats, likes, checking checks. Independent States of One.

So, of course, whose phone should loudly proclaim with

parping horns an incoming text at that moment, but his own? Even the woman with the stubs glanced round. He was going to have to work out how to change his settings.

'Sorry.' He dragged the phone from his pocket before the horns could parp again and held it at arm's length and angled away from the sun. Was that…? It was. Beth. *Coming back for a bit. That OK?* The box on the crossing beeped. The people around him stepped out on to the road. He followed a couple of paces behind, texting as he walked, trusting to spellcheck to compensate for clumsy thumbs. *Be lovely to see you.* Then almost as an afterthought, *When were you thinking?*

He stopped on the other side, watching the pulsing ellipsis of his daughter's reply in the making. *Plane boards in 30 mins.*

He turned around and pressed the button for the Green Man again.

An open-topped tour bus came between him and the lights facing, half empty, or maybe, given the early hour, half full.

'We just passed the SSE Arena. On your right now, the famous Harland and Wolff cranes, Samson and Goliath, an early attempt at power-sharing in Belfast…'

Beth hadn't been across since her granny's funeral – a year and a half ago now: morning flight in, evening flight out – and before that it was… When? Not since he had been in this house, that's for sure. There had been plans, but, well, she was a hundred kinds of busy, something always came up. He never pressed her. 'Totally understand,' he would say. The busy-ness, he meant, rather than the business. Promotions. He had been imagining music festivals to begin with when it seemed he should have been seeing people dressed as blackcurrants handing out soft drinks in train stations and shopping malls, and actually the odd music festival too. She had chopped and changed a bit the first few years, jumping from one moving train to one moving even faster was how she had described it herself, but seemed well settled now. Well thought of too. There had been talk (when had they last talked about work?) of a partnership in the firm she was with. She was getting together the deposit on a flat of her own. In central London.

First thing he did when he got back to the house was push the shoeboxes into the dead corner of the spare room with the Sean archive and cover the whole lot with a bedspread. He unrolled the futon mattress and had to back out of the room to allow the dust he raised to settle. When he came back, he weighted the corners with books while he ran the vacuum over it. A bit better. Floor looked worse, mind you. He vacuumed it too then lifted down the anglepoise lamp from the top of the wardrobe, only remembering as he plugged it in and thumbed the switch that the reason it was up there in the first place was that he hadn't got round to mending the fuse... because – another ten minutes of hoking in drawers – he didn't have a fuse to mend it with. Bollocks.

At the last minute he raced round to M&S. He seriously didn't think he was up to Brian. He took his six items to the till at the end furthest from his. A woman he had never seen before, though it was in the nature of the job and the uniform that he knew at once her name was Louise. White-haired – prematurely, he wanted to say, but even on that first glance he could nearly not imagine what other colour it could ever have been. She passed his ready meals, his salad, his cheesecake and his Scottish strawberries over the scanner. It was as though he had never seen that before either. Never seen *hands* before. He was conscious suddenly of staring. Conscious of her being conscious of it.

She drew her hands back, folded one inside the other next to the money drawer.

'Cash or card?' she asked, something told him not for the first time.

'I'm so sorry,' he said. 'I was just, I don't know, miles away… Card.'

She took it and a moment later gave it back.

'Receipt?'

'No thank you.'

She nodded, looked past him. 'Who's next there, please?'

The taxi was turning into the street as he reached through the front gate to raise the latch. He opened the door, set the shopping in the hall and waited. The driver was leaning forward, counting down the numbers with his index finger: forty-five, forty-three, forty-one, thirty-nine – Bingo! – he lit on Herbie finally. Beth dipped her head as she paid the man, then stepped out. He caught himself repeating under his breath what his own father had said the first time he laid eyes on her in the maternity hospital, twenty-seven years ago: Egg 1 Sperm 0.

'I look awful, don't I?' She grabbed handfuls of hair, trying to restore the volume the airplane cabin pressure had robbed it of.

'I was just thinking how well you were looking.' Too thin, but when did he not think so? He came back down the path to meet her. She brought her cheek up close to his, circled him with her arms without any part of their bodies touching. The girl whose hugs had used to hit him like a cannonball.

'Are you forgetting something?' The taxi driver had got out and popped his boot.

'What am I like?'

She went back and collected her bag from him. The same army kit bag Herbie had carried into the departures lounge for her the night she left home.

'You know you can always come back if it doesn't work out.'

'I know,' she said, 'but it will.' And it had.

The driver tooted his horn in parting. Beth waved.

'He was telling me he used to have an aunt lived down this street. He practically lived here himself during the school holidays. Just as well, I wouldn't have had a clue.' She looked up at the front. 'Would it put you in mind of Granny's house a wee bit?'

'Almost brick-for-brick identical.'

WHERE ARE WE NOW?

She nodded. 'It's nice.' Then as though he had contradicted her, 'No, it is, it's really nice.'

'Wasn't a big lot needed done, which was part of the attraction for me.'

Inside now, the lower part of the knock-through, with its armchair and two-seater sofa and the television he hadn't yet got round to replacing with a flatter screen.

'Cosy,' she said.

He picked up her bag. 'I can't believe you still have this.'

'Oh, no, that's not that one.'

'It's very like it.'

'I suppose it is.'

A moment. Neither spoke.

'Will I put it up in your room?'

'I have my own room?'

'Where did you think you were going to sleep?'

'I don't know… the sofa?'

They looked at it together. It seemed to sag under the scrutiny.

'Right.' He hoisted the bag on to his shoulder. He would have sworn it was the same one.

She stayed a step behind him the whole way up the stairs, down the short landing.

'Here you are.' He opened the door, leaning in with it to let her pass.

'I remember that lamp!' She tapped it and it genuflected. She pressed her hands flat together beneath her nose, bowed in reply. 'Venerable Giver of Light.'

'It needs a fuse.' Herbie was at the wardrobe. 'There's plenty of hangers,' rattling them. He turned. 'How long are you able to stay?'

'It sort of depends.' She went and tilted the wooden blinds, down then up again. 'Where's your loo?'

'Downstairs, through the kitchen. Light's on the hall side of the door.'

'It *is* like Granny's.'

He used the time that she was in there to fill the kettle and lift down a couple of mugs.

'You've no bath,' she said when she came back into the kitchen.

'The people that were here before me took it out.' He couldn't say he'd missed it up to now.

'Pity.'

And it came back to him, all at once, the long soaks she and Tanya used to take – together when Beth was small, and, even when she had outgrown that, both following the same routine. Lavender oil. Scented candles. Classic FM. Balm, Tanya would say, for the troubled soul.

'Coffee? Tea? I have, let's see, ordinary, and mint, in at the back here somewhere.'

'Actually, I think I'll maybe go and lie down for a while.' She dragged her fingers down her face, widening the dark rings under her eyes. 'I had to be up at five this morning to get to the airport on time.'

'Of course, of course, go on ahead,' he said and put her mug away again and then a moment later his too.

He sat for a long while in the silence she left when she went upstairs, a little dazed by the entire morning's turn of events. If it hadn't been for the faint smell of perfume he could nearly have persuaded himself that she hadn't been there at all.

She slept in the end till past six o'clock. (She could sleep for Ireland, that girl, wasn't that what they had always said? Sleep for Britain too.) Got up, showered. Another forty-five minutes. He could actually have had something made instead of buying in ready meals, looking like he didn't know how. He paused in the act of peeling back the plastic film of a chicken supreme – of watching his hands peel back the plastic film – and realised he was blushing. He had stared at that woman on the till. Louise. And then his apology… attempted apology. Dear God. He wanted to go back round and say sorry properly: I am not a man who stares, honestly. To which she would say what? *Oh, right, so I just got lucky?*

Maybe the reason he had never seen her wasn't that she had just started but that she only worked the morning shift. And, really, how often was he there in the early part of the day? Hardly ever.

Beth still had a towel on her head when they sat down at the table.

'Do you mind?' she asked.

'Not at all. Like old times.'

'Minus Mum.'

35

'Well, yes, there's that.'

They ate a while in silence. 'Did you know you've a wee leak in your shower tray?' she said then. 'Corner nearest the door. Futon's comfortable, though. Where was that out of?'

'A place over on the Lisburn Road. It's gone now.'

'Really comfortable.'

They ate.

'This chicken is lovely.'

'Marks.'

'I know, but still.'

Another minute passed of more or less silent chewing and swallowing. Herbie cleared his mouth, set his fork on his plate. 'So…'

'Tell me about your job,' Beth said quickly.

'Mine? Job's maybe too big a word. I'm only contracted for seven and a half hours.'

'But you go in more than that…'

'The freelance stuff? It's a little bit in the lap of the gods, but this time of the year, yeah, it can get pretty busy all right.'

'And is it still in that wreck of a place on… what's this you call it?'

'Balmoral Avenue?' That's right, there had been a time when she was at school, some history project she was doing, he had taken her there thinking they kept old newspapers. A hodgepodge, it was then, of Edwardian red brick, Elizabeth II concrete and Troubles-stalwart prefabs. And barbed wire, of course: barbed wire in abundance. None of which prevented the bombers getting through eventually. 'No, they moved it four or five years ago, Titanic Quarter, brand-new building down by the Visitors' Centre.'

'Is that not a bit like putting sweeties next to the till?' she said. 'Family trees *and* maritime disasters?'

'It gets worse – you know they're filming that *Game of Thrones* down there now as well? Huge big shed of a studio.'

'Oh, God, the two women in front of me on the plane, that's all they talked about. I think they were actually expecting to find boars and direwolves roaming the streets.'

'There are hotels too, and they're building more. Fella I know calls it the Bermuda Shorts Triangle.' That was Brian. He was quoting Brian, who wasn't, in fairness, on this occasion, stretching a point all that far.

The tourists who weren't already trapped there hopped, in their dozens, off the tour buses that stopped every thirty minutes at the Records Office door. Few if any of them could have had the first idea what a tithe applotment was or suspected that was where their ancestors might be lurking.

'And you?' He had been biding his time. 'How are things?'

Beth picked up the plates – 'Leave those,' he said – then set them down again. Gently.

'Things?' She laughed. Then sighed. 'Things have gone a bit...' She searched for the words. Seemed bemused at the paucity of choice. 'A bit off the rails lately, if I'm being totally honest.'

'How off the rails?'

'You'll not be mad?'

He reached for her hand, which eluded him.

'I'm bankrupt.' She picked up the plates again and walked with them, before he had time to react, into the kitchen.

He stared, stupefied, at the empty chair a moment, then got up and followed her to the door. 'What do you mean you're bankrupt?'

'I mean I didn't have enough money to pay my debts.'

He was trying to think if he had actually heard her properly last time they talked, when she had used the word 'partner'.

'But hold on a minute…'

She turned from the sink where she had set the plates. 'What?'

Her sharpness of movement, and tongue, threw him.

'You never said anything.' Could he have sounded any more pathetic? 'I would have helped.'

Another laugh, shorter even than the last, harsher. 'I don't think so, Dad. Not with these debts. Anyway' – she had reined herself in a bit – 'it's done now.' Just like that. 'It's really not as big a deal as you think. You can apply for it online. It only takes about half an hour. Twelve months' time, I'll be completely discharged.'

There were so many questions.

'So that kit bag?'

So many questions and he chose that? But it *was* the one she had taken away with her, he was certain of it now.

'Is one of my few remaining worldly possessions and contains pretty much all the rest.' She dried her hands on a tea towel. Smiled tightly. 'Could we maybe not talk about this any more tonight?'

That tone. He had, not forgotten, exactly, just not had cause to remember it or the efforts – he and Tanya working in relay or in tandem – to keep the shutters from coming down completely.

'Why don't we just leave those dishes? Do them in the morning,' he said. 'I'll make us some tea.'

They watched TV for a while, 'in real time,' Beth said, 'imagine!' Nearly every programme had people being voted out, or in, or otherwise measured and weighed against one another.

These things crept in like the tide, he knew. You could channel hop around it for a while, but eventually, wherever you turned, there was just no escape.

The news for once was almost a relief.

The lead story on the local bulletin was the missed deadline in the talks aimed at getting the power-sharing executive back up and running. 'Oh, wait,' said Beth, 'this one *is* a repeat. Next episode, dancing in the street, ring the church bells, history has been made! Again.'

'Couldn't see the place far enough,' was what Tanya had said to him, that night – Beth's eighteenth birthday – when she announced she intended to leave the moment her A Levels were over, not even hanging about for the results. 'You could hardly blame her.'

Tanya herself went a bare month after that. 'It just feels like the end of a chapter,' she said. 'Do you not think?'

Herbie hadn't quite got there yet. He always had been slower at reading things. (Nights in bed, his chin on her shoulder as she licked a finger to turn the pages of her magazine. 'Wait, wait, I'm not finished!') But he was far enough along to know she wasn't altogether wrong.

The weather forecast for tomorrow was pretty decent again. That was what the shrunken-suited man-child standing before the weather map actually said: 'Another pretty decent day in prospect.' Like today. The sun coming out as he crossed the Dee Street Bridge, slipping off his jacket.

He sat forward. 'Here, do you remember the time we went blackberry picking in the Titanic Quarter?'

'*What?*'

'Well, it was still the shipyard then, technically. One summer, you were, I don't know, ten or eleven maybe.'

She turned around, knees pulled up, cushion to her chest.

'The place was a bit of a wasteland: hadn't been an actual ship built in years. There were these huge brambles growing out through one of the gates, big old green wrought-iron things.'

'Oh, *yeah*,' she said, sounding as if she wanted to let herself be convinced.

'And the blackberries… The two of us must have picked half a bucketful between us in about ten minutes.'

'And how were they?'

'Dusty, even after they were washed. Right down between the little' – he didn't know the word – 'polyps… blobs. I think we managed to salvage a handful to throw into an apple pie.'

'Where did we get the apples –' she thumped her cushion, boom-boom, 'the *gasworks?*'

He nodded: very good. 'I was just thinking,' he said, 'that's where I was standing today when I got your text.'

'No!'

'There's a road goes off to the left, which is how I remember the spot, because of course they took down the gates when they started all the big building work. I always wondered how the brambles grew up so quickly, then it occurred to me, maybe they had been there all along, you know, from before the shipyard even, just sort of biding their time... Like, there was a thing on the radio the other week, these geese that come from Canada to a tiny patch of grass somewhere up the Shankill every winter. The people on the street come out and feed them, make sure nobody tries to do anything to them. They reckon they have probably been coming since that whole area was countryside.'

'Welcome to sunny Shankill Road. Imagine how disappointed the young ones are when they see where their parents have brought them... *Where's the water?*'

'Shankill Leisure Centre.'

'Chicks go half price.'

Her eyes drifted back to the TV.

'That's a lovely thought,' she said, after a minute. 'Underground blackberries.' Another minute. She started to laugh, lowered her voice, bearded it, '*We haven't gone away, you know.*'

She stopped, returned from her brief sojourn in Gerry Adams. Herbie looked at her face side on, chin resting on the cushion clutched to her chest. His daughter the bankrupt.

3

Geese came and went, but seagulls in Belfast were perpetual. There was one in particular that stood vigil on a bollard across the road from the Records Office: a great black back was the informed opinion, the Vincent Price of seagulls, a single red mark on the lower part of its cruel-looking beak like an indelible drip of blood, and a one-eyed sideways stare that could chill you to the marrow. For the past few weeks it had been even more unnerving and aggressive than usual. Hungry too. There wasn't a crisp or a crumb dropped within a fifty-yard radius but the seagull swooped down and claimed it. One of the security women had had a sandwich snatched right out of her hand as she prepared to take a bite. (Piri-piri chicken. The seagull swallowed it like it was a fresh-caught herring.) Pete, another of the freelancers, had his baseball cap plucked clean off his head, chewed and hawked back up.

Gulled.

Kansas City Royals, the cap was. Even online they were hard to get. It had cost him the best part of thirty quid. In the old days, he told the company that had gathered to marvel and to gag at the regurgitated mess, someone would have come round by now and dealt with that bird.

'Wait' – this was Lydia – 'you're not talking like a punishment attack?'

'I'm not saying it's right, but I mean they done a dog once that was running round our way buck mad, snapping at people, chasing cars up and down the street. The council weren't doing a thing about it. A child could have been bitten, or some driver could have lost control of his car, ploughed into a whole crowd of pedestrians, the front of somebody's house, maybe, while they were all sitting watching the TV.'

'Simple civic-mindedness is what you're saying.'

Lydia started singing, 'I've seen everything, I've seen everything,' and the forty-somethings among them fell to trying to remember who that was by – not the Housemartins, though it had a Housemartinsy vibe…

The seagull wasn't there when Herbie arrived – at the third time of asking that week – the next morning. (Not a sound from behind Beth's door before he left.) Maybe it had finally taken the hint from all the people doing crucifix arm signs at it and flapped right off.

The doors of the Records Office had only been open ten minutes, but already a queue had formed in the lobby of tourists waiting for their visitors' passes. For this, above all else, had some of them travelled several thousand miles, spent months online into the wee small hours of their faraway days fantasising about what they might find. A connection to the United Irishmen and the doomed rebellion in the name of the union of Catholic, Protestant and Dissenter was the ultimate in desirability, although any defiance of authority, spiritual or temporal, was a retrofitted feather in a far-off family's cap.

One by one they would be made to sit in the chair to the right of the reception desk and told to look into the camera, which to their evident and understandable surprise was housed in a ball attached CCTV-wise to the ceiling. It gave them all the air of people captured – and realising in that instant, *shit*, that they had been captured – in the act of holding up a filling station.

A couple at the back of the queue were discussing the poem etched on a bronze panel above the door. 'I take my stand by the Ulster names/ Each clean hard name like a weathered stone…'

'Seamus Heaney,' one of them pronounced confidently and the woman with her nodded. Herbie resisted the temptation of saying other local poets were available, not least because, truly, how many could he name from wherever it was (South Africa? Zimbabwe?) they were from?

Lydia came in a quarter of an hour behind him. She took the seat at the table next to him. Leaned in close.

'Guess what.'

'What?'

'That fucking seagull.'

'What about it?'

'It's a mammy.' That would certainly account for the more frenzied than usual feeding of late. 'I just saw the chick, if you could call it that: not much more than a furry egg on legs,

45

only squawking. And of course the mammy's looking at it like it's the pinnacle of Creation. Pete was right, we should have done something while we had the chance. Can't touch it now.'

'I thought you were all for leaving it be.'

'Yeah, when there was just it.'

'I have a feeling that in order for there to be a chick there had to be more than just it.'

'Even worse. They mate for life, don't they? That bollard is going to be like a family inheritance, yea, even on to the ninth and tenth generation. We might as well run up the white flag now, lay down our lunches and favourite online purchases.'

Another fifteen minutes, and Pete came in. 'Did you hear?'

'I already told him,' Lydia said.

'I think we should get up a petition.'

'Who to?'

'I don't know. The Titanic Foundation, the Harbour Commissioners.'

A shortish man in a freshly pressed white shirt had presented himself at the enquiries desk. He turned now as the receptionist pointed out Herbie.

'I'm sorry to have to break this up, but that's my ten o'clock appointment.'

Lydia cast an eye over him. 'A real live nephew of Uncle Sam's?'

'All the way from Tampa, Florida.'

'Ex army?'

'Major, United States Marine Corps, retired.'

WHERE ARE WE NOW?

Lydia turned to Pete. 'There's your chance,' she said. 'I'm sure he had to deal with worse than a great black back gull in his day.'

'I'm sorry, but I still have some principles. Even for that seagull I'll have no truck with the US military–industrial complex.'

Herbie had the task – pleasant, he had fancied in advance – of explaining to the major that his own great-to-the-power-of-eight grandfather had in all likelihood come from Florida.

'No, no,' the major said, 'he went *to* Florida.'

'I know, but he came from there too.' He had the frame lined up and waiting in the microfiche. 'Look, this is him...' The tip of Herbie's middle finger on the screen was nearly as wide as the silvery line of great-eight-granddaddy's name. 'St Mary's Church, parish of Kilmud, paid a tithe of a pound of meal. St Mary's was the estate church of Florida Manor.'

He recalled hearing Sean Copeland mention in one of his client consultations a Loyal Florida Infantry Yeomanry, which had been raised in 1798 to suppress the United Irishmen in that part of County Down. This was maybe not the optimum moment to mention that.

The major took out a pair of rimless glasses from a slender stainless-steel case that looked as though it had seen service in tougher theatres of operation than this, peered, took them off again, stopped just short of replacing them in their case. 'It says all that there?'

He sounded suspicious. He sounded as though he thought

he might be being short-changed. Florida to Florida. It seemed, rather than delightful coincidence, just way too convenient.

'The manor house is still there, out Killinchy direction,' Herbie said.

The major had his glasses back on, leaning into the angled hood of the microfiche reader. 'Killinchy.' He sounded a good deal less certain about the Ulster names than the poet.

'Wouldn't be more than half an hour's drive.'

'Is that part of the service?' The major straightened, hitched his belt. Herbie was beginning to wonder whether Marine Corps was cover for other more specialist duties. 'Or am I going to have to pay you extra?'

Herbie left the major with the numbers of two local cab companies and a promise that he would only bill up to 10.24, the exact minute when he got up and walked out into the landing to take three very deep breaths and tell himself, really, Herbie, you don't need any of this.

He knocked off four of his seven and a half hours collecting documents from the reading room and returning them to their allotted places in the store before calling it a day. The seagull, sure enough, was pacing backwards and forwards in front of its bollard, seemingly torn between wanting to show the chick off and – wings angling out gunslinger-swift from its body – warning passersby not to even think of coming within ten feet of it.

The chick swayed on its thin legs, grey-brown down buffeted by the breeze coming in low and hard off Belfast

Lough, head turning this way and that, black eye working overtime. So, this is the world?

Squawk!

The first few days she was with him, Beth barely crossed the front doorstep. When she wasn't sleeping, from what he could tell, she was sitting on the sofa, motionless but for her thumb on the phone screen, a glass of water with a slice of lemon in it at her feet.

'Why don't you at least go out into the yard?' he asked her at last.

The people before him had kept tortoises, at some distant point in the past, or perhaps – even more distantly – the people before them had. Whichever of them had left it, there was a – 'run' couldn't be the word – 'crawl', then, all along the left-hand yard wall. The wood was perished and the wire in the few places where it was still intact entirely rusted. The base was stone effect, contoured to provide entertainment or challenge. A couple of the deeper depressions had filled with rain, becoming watery tombs for the slaters who had moved in en masse when the tortoises moved out.

Herbie had put it off and put it off (the slater dead, if you must know, rain-bleached and inverted and resembling nothing so much as lumps of porridge in someone else's sink) then finally got round to paying someone to come and clear the thing out the weekend after Easter. Where the cage had been he put a bench that Sam had found for him on Gumtree, a bit of trellising facing it to train wisteria and encourage it – at long last – to bloom, in glorious early Seventies purple, which was the problem, apparently. The bloom not the colour.

'Hay fever,' Beth said, 'remember?'

'I thought that was all cleared up.'

She sniffed, drily. 'It comes and goes.'

He asked her if there were maybe friends she wanted to catch up with, people from school, or... or (who had she used to chum around with?), you know, wherever. They were welcome to call round, he could take himself off upstairs, no bother.

'I'm fine as I am,' she said and – a sip from the glass – went back to thumbing her phone.

They took their meals (and truth be told he was glad of the time alone in the kitchen making them). They watched TV. They said good night and closed their doors.

The fourth day, he came home to find the house empty and a note on the kitchen countertop. 'Away into town. I'll do dinner.'

She came back an hour and a half later with a bag brimful of leeks and a face on her like thunder.

'You know that big long row of murals at the bottom of the road there?'

He did indeed. A four-panel – make that '-gable' – justification for an organisation that had spent its 'war' years murdering Catholics. 'Freedom Corner, they call it.'

'Yeah, right,' she said. She pulled open the fridge door and began to transfer the leeks from the bag to the salad drawer, pausing every now and then to wag one as she spoke. 'I just passed a group of tourists taking photos of each other in front of it. Big cheesy smiles, like they were –' she shook a leek in impotent rage, 'I don't know where… Universal's Islands of Adventure. I mean, have you seen what they have written up there?'

'I can't say I pay it much heed.'

'"Tomorrow belongs to us." Do the people who did that not know what that sounds like, or do they just not care? I mean, you don't have to have been brought up on *Cabaret* for the little Nazi alarm bells to ring. And those tourists, do they think it's *funny*, posing with that?'

Maybe, probably not, anyone's guess.

She pushed the salad drawer shut, with difficulty. 'There's no more room in your fridge,' she said and left the bag on the floor before it, still three leeks shy of empty. She sat at the table and took out her phone. 'I tried to get a photo of those people' – squinting – 'nah, it's come out all blurry.' Tossing her phone – the entire subject – on the table, 'My Uber driver was saying he knows you.'

'Uber?'

'It's like a taxi.'

'I know what it is, but what are you doing using it?'

'Well, it's way cheaper than a taxi if that's what you mean.'

'Not as cheap as the bus that goes past the end of the street.'

'My feet were sore. I'd a big bag of leeks, in case you hadn't noticed.'

'We have a fruit and veg shop round the corner.'

'I didn't go into town for leeks. I went in and I saw them. They had them reduced. That whole bag for two pounds. Jesus Christ, Dad, do I have to justify everything. I went in to get out. It was you that was telling me to.'

He didn't let himself say anything more, though she left him the time to, daring him. Gave up finally.

'He says you come into the cafe he goes to.'

The Uber driver, he guessed she meant.

'What's his name?'

She picked up the phone again, checked the app. 'Paul.'

'I can't think of any… Wait, about your age?'

She didn't take the calculation well. 'I'd have said a bit older.'

'Glasses?'

'Well, he was wearing shades, but I guess they could have been prescription. Brown hair, side parting, thinnish face.'

'Sounds like him, but I don't know what he'd be doing driving a taxi.'

'Uber.'

'Right. I thought he was with Diageo.'

'Not today he wasn't. What's this he said the place was called the two of you go to?'

'Sam's.'

'That's it. He says you're never usually out of the place…'

'I wouldn't go as far as that.'

She tilted her head, narrowed one eye. 'You're not embarrassed of me, are you?'

'Don't be silly. I just thought… I mean, you didn't seem…'

He stopped. Sometimes it was just better to. Start again: 'Tell you what, seeing as you still have your jacket on…'

She thought a moment. 'Maybe.' A moment more. 'All right, yeah, that would be nice.'

He held the front door open for her.

'Are you sure you don't want to call a taxi?'

'I knew you wouldn't be able to let it go. I just knew it.'

Paul, in fact, was just about to get into his car, parked in the lay-by in front of the cafe, takeaway coffee balanced on the roof while he searched for his keys. Glasses now rather than shades.

'There he's there,' said Beth.

'So, it was you,' Herbie said.

Paul patted himself down for verification now rather than keys. 'It still is, I hope.'

'I was telling Beth you were with Diageo.'

'I was.'

'What happened?'

'You would have to ask Diageo that.' He opened the car door, sat in the driver's seat. 'This is just to tide me over. You have to keep busy, don't you?'

'Here.' Beth lifted the coffee cup off the roof. 'Don't be forgetting this.'

'Thanks,' Paul said. He was swapping over to the sunglasses again. He looked like he was getting ready to go skiing. 'And for the rating. Enjoy your leeks.'

Sam himself was behind the cafe door, putting up an A4 poster on the inside facing out. 'Thursday Night is Music

Night'. Grand piano, crotchets and quavers spiralling away from it into the top left corner, an open wine bottle in the bottom right next to the letters BYO. The design boat had not been pushed out very far.

'I thought we'd give it a whirl,' he said when Herbie and Beth were finally able to step inside, 'see how it went.' He had found a wee lad, living up a lane somewhere in the Craigantlet Hills, who played jazz piano. 'You've got to see him, complete time warp: wing-tipped shoes and Oxford bags. Was quoting Gershwin to me: "songs for girls in love to hum on fire escapes on hot summer nights".'

'You don't see too many fire escapes out in the Craigantlet Hills,' Herbie said.

'Can't knock it for an ambition, all the same,' said Beth and Sam looked at her properly for the first time.

'Sorry,' Herbie said, 'my daughter, Beth.'

'Daughter?'

'Don't tell me he never mentioned me?'

'Oh, he did, but you look nothing like him... A bullet dodged.'

'I was about to ask you if we had to book for the BYO night,' said Herbie, 'but I've suddenly gone off the idea.'

'Stick me down anyway,' Beth said. 'Plus guest.'

Derek came out and they did the introductions all over again, and another version of the bullet being dodged.

'You two really need to work on your script,' Herbie told them.

'I like your Scrabble letters,' said Beth.

'Thank you,' Derek said, though more to Sam, who shrugged.

'You know, though, someone has moved the D and C...?'

Derek was out from behind the counter. 'I keep thinking whoever's doing that will grow out of it.'

'I keep telling him not to hold his breath,' Sam said.

'So,' Beth asked the moment they were out the door, coffee drunk, world watched as it went by, 'are Sam and Derek...?'

'Yep.'

'And nobody...?'

'Nope.'

'There's hope.'

They walked the few yards to the pedestrian crossing. 'You won't take this the wrong way?'

'That pretty much guarantees I will.'

She squeezed his arm. 'It's strange seeing you with other people. I'm not used to it.'

'No?'

'You always seemed to me a bit... I don't mean stand-offish, but you didn't really bother much, isn't that what they say?' She nodded, satisfied with the formulation. 'Neither of yous did. I know Mum had her gang from school, but how often did they all get back – once a year? And the rest of the time... I just can't think.'

Herbie opened his mouth to protest. Closed it again. He didn't know that she was altogether wrong. He simply could no longer get enough of a purchase on that period of his life to say for sure. There had been evenings in neighbours' houses

– and neighbours in Oriel (seriously, what *had* they been thinking?) – a group of eight, all of an age, or at least a stage, small kids, big mortgages – but they had never developed a pattern, never mind a routine. Two of the couples had moved away – *on*, was his impression – Beth might still have been in nursery school – and the remaining couple, at the far end of the street, became once-yearly visitors, one of the nights between Christmas and New Year, and then, as the penny finally dropped that the four who had gone had been the glue, not even that.

They must have heard about him and Tanya or at the very least seen the 'For Sale' sign go up – it was out there long enough before it turned to 'Sold' – but they didn't come near him once, although he supposed, looked at from their end, it was him didn't come near them.

Just didn't bother.

There was an epitaph.

Monday night was leek and bean hash, Tuesday night leek and lemon fettuccine, Wednesday night Monday night's leftovers served on a bed of Tuesday night's. Thursday night they made leek soup and stuck it in the freezer before heading out for some much-needed leek respite.

They stopped in on the way at the off-licence, where Herbie took longer than he normally would, or his budget normally merited, over the choice of wine, being flusher than anticipated by £50 thanks to the descendant of Terence Quin, currently resident in Hong Kong, who earlier that afternoon discovered to her delight that her distant ancestor had been entered in the annals for turning up drunk at church to receive his alms on a Sunday in May 1792. God knows what sort of a tip the woman would have given him if the bold Terence had succeeded in his attempt to undo his breeches.

The piano was upright rather than grand. Sam and Derek had still had to lose two tables to get it in, although they had filled all the rest, could easily, they said, have filled them twice over. The staff from the Post Office were there, all seated together, all appearing to have Brought Their Own and one for a friend. People on the edge, of opportunity or hardship, they seemed undecided which, but ready to drink to the one or in defiance of the other. Beth and Herbie had Emmet and Yolanda to one side of them. Beth asked, without waiting for a further steer, if they were from around here. Emmet told her he and his brother ran the wheelie-bin cleaning service that did pretty much the whole of the area. Yolanda told her she ran Emmet and his brother. 'They would be clueless otherwise, the pair of them.'

Derek appeared. 'Can I open that for you?' he said and Herbie handed him the wine. The corkscrew was embossed with the name of a restaurant in the Cornish town of Looe. Or more probably no longer in the Cornish town of Looe.

Herbie filled Beth's glass and his own ('This is for you, Terence Quin,' he said inside his head) and seeing Emmet's was empty offered to pour him one too.

'Don't mind if I do.'

Yolanda covered her glass with her hand. 'Driving, but thank you.'

She drank nothing stronger than fizzy water, but still seemed to become more garrulous with every glass she put away. Halfway through her third, while the musical entertainment was still courtesy of iTunes, she had an arm draped round Emmet's neck, saying, go on, go on, tell them, when you were at school, what did you play…?

'I played the oboe.'

'And what did your da call it?'

'The oboy,' said Emmet, sheepishly.

Yolanda positively hooted. 'Every single time he took it out: Oboy!'

'For three years,' Emmet said.

'Until he just stopped taking it out altogether… Didn't you?' Stroking Emmet's ear with her thumb, 'I'll bet you could still get a toot or two out of it… I mean, if someone was to come and stick one in your hand.'

She turned in her chair to mock-frown at Beth, who hadn't said a word. 'You've a dirty mind, you.'

'Yolanda,' Emmet said, 'that's Herbie's daughter.'

Herbie's daughter put the back of her hand to her forehead. 'My innocence snatched from me!'

The only other oboyist in his year, Emmet told them, toured America with the Ulster Youth Orchestra then went on to the Royal Northern College of Music in Manchester, got through however many auditions for second chair oboe with the Hallé Orchestra there – his parents, 'ordinary working

WHERE ARE WE NOW?

people, like you and me,' said Emmet, were speechless with
pride...

'The mother not so much,' said Yolanda. 'She never shut up
about it.'

But then her son got in with a crowd who were running
raves – 'Those were like outdoor dances the youth used to
have,' Yolanda, translating from the Eighties, said for Beth's
benefit, 'way before your time, and mine' – 'And that,' said
Emmet, 'was the last anyone heard of chairs at the Hallé or
anything else to do with his oboe.'

'Until,' said Yolanda under her breath.

'Who's telling this story?' Emmet asked her, and she held
up her hands, So arrest me! 'Until,' he said, 'about five years
later this record came out with this little bit of a sample...' He
whistled it.

'No!' said Beth. 'That was him? The Volvo ad?'

'Volvo ad, Olympic opening ceremony...'

'Recorded in his student digs,' Yolanda said to Beth, and to
Emmet, 'you always leave that bit out.'

He nodded. 'That's right. In his digs, when he was nineteen.
Mucking about with a friend's DAT machine. And he probably
made more money out of that...'

'Or DAT...' (Yolanda, quietly, almost apologetically.)

'... than he would have if he had been sitting in the second
chair at the Hallé from that day to this.'

'You know what the old folks say,' said Yolanda.

'Only from *Pulp Fiction*, but yes.'

'"*C'est la vie.*"'

'Indeed.'

Sam and Derek had gone for an economy-class in-flight menu choice, chicken or pasta, take-it-or-leave-it chocolate brownie for dessert. There was a raffle ticket paper-clipped to every menu card, free entry. The prizes – listed on the specials board – were in the same cheerfully plain vein as the menu. A bottle of white wine, a bottle of red, two soda and two wheaten from the home bakery, five pounds off your next purchase from the fish and chip saloon, and why not, there were still another six nights in the week in which to eat when Sam's had shut its doors for the day. Two columns the prizes ran to. It would be an unlucky table that won nothing at all.

The wee lad from the Craigantlet Hills came on as the main course was being served. He was called – had, unlikely as it seemed, always been called – Kurtis Bain. He looked, despite the wingtips and the Oxford bags, about fourteen. He sounded, when he sat down at the piano, let his fingers stray up and down the keys a couple of times, and started – eyes closed, lids trembling – to sing, about seventy-five. ''S wonderful, 's marvellous, you should care for me, 's awful nice, 's paradise, 's what I love to see...'

He had the whole thing down pat, but heartfelt.

There was a girl sitting alone at a table to the right of the piano, bow-fronted blouse, hair in perfectly executed finger waves, who appeared, from the way she kept trying to angle it, to be recording the entire set on her phone, which in her hands looked like the anachronism. It was a while even so before Herbie twigged (the third verse of 'Aren't You Kinda Glad We Did?' to be precise, with its wouldn'ts, couldn'ts and shouldn'ts) that Kurtis Bain was addressing all his songs to her.

He stood up from the piano after the eighth, bowed with his hands clasped back to back between his thighs, and went and sat by her side while Derek and Sam took centre stage.

'If you can contain your excitement, ladies and gentlemen,' Sam said, 'eyes down for this evening's raffle!'

Derek shook the bag, Sam drew the tickets.

Yolanda won the bottle of red wine first number out. 'That's my Saturday night sorted then!' Two full columns later, Beth won the final prize, a ticket to the home of the local intermediate football team. 'This would be a good time to go,' Emmet said.

'Is the football season not over?' Beth asked.

'That's what I mean.'

Plates were cleared, the take-it-or-leave-it brownies were served, bottles over and beyond what the doctor had ordered were opened. Kurtis Bain had just come back on and was warming to 'Waiting for the Sun to Come Out' when Paul came in. Staggered. He looked a mess. A graze ran the length of his nose. Blood had dripped on to his shirtfront. Beth stood up.

'Are you OK?'

Yolanda opened out her wheelchair and Paul sank down into it. Or it was the other way round: Paul was sinking and Yolanda's quick thinking arrested his fall. It all happened so fast it was possible nobody else in the cafe had even noticed. His hands were shaking as he took his glasses off. One of the lenses fell out on to his lap.

'Some fella…' he struggled for the words, '…down behind the picture house…'

He's been beaten up, Herbie thought.

'… ran into the side of me.'

'You were in a *car crash*?' Yolanda said. 'For God's sake somebody phone him an ambulance.'

Beth already had two nines up on her screen before Paul stopped her. 'I'm all right.'

'You don't look it.'

'You do not,' said Beth.

'How's the car?' Emmet the Practical.

'I had to climb out over the passenger's seat.' Paul screwed his eyes tight shut at the thought of how close he had been to greater harm. 'The driver's door is completely banjaxed.'

Yolanda moved a glass of water towards him. 'You need to let the police know at the very least.'

'I don't think so.'

Something in his tone, the quick glance towards the door… 'Who was it hit you?' Herbie asked.

'He didn't give me his name, only his rank.' Paul managed at the third attempt to get the lens back in its frame. 'Apparently he's a brigadier.'

'A soldier?' Beth asked, and they all looked at her: where have you been? (England, of course, the best part of ten years.) 'Oh. Right. That sort of brigadier.'

'He told me he could provide half a dozen witnesses who would say it was my fault. He could provide someone with a freshly broken leg, or arm, or collarbone, or fucking spine if need be, who would say they were in the passenger seat beside him.'

'Just learn to sing and never mope,' Kurtis Bain sang, 'there is a thing that's known as hope.'

Paul seemed to notice him for the first time. He looked for a moment utterly bewildered. Who was that? *What* was that?

'Come on, up you get,' Yolanda said, and took his place in the chair. 'I'll give you a lift home – you can get your car in the morning.'

Paul shook his head. 'It might as well just sit there, for all the use it is to me now.'

Kurtis Bain's fingers pranced. 'Dreary are the flowers, weary are the hours, waiting for the sun to come out.'

Yolanda was gone half an hour. Emmet jumped up to get the door for her.

'That poor fella,' she said.

'Is he really shaken?'

'Tell you the God's honest truth, I was nearly going to drive on up to A&E despite him. I watched him as he climbed up his stairs… He lives over his brother's garage, did you know that? Or it's his brother's now, but it used to be the whole family's, when the parents were alive. Weird set-up, if you ask me. He had to shout down to me to put a pound in the electricity meter before he could get the lights on. Must have spilt all his change clambering out of his car.'

'Wait, the meter's not even in his own flat?' Emmet asked.

'It's on the garage wall next to the deckchairs. I near fell out of this flipping thing trying to reach it. I told him he was going to need more than a pound. I rapped the brother's door. I could hear the television – I could hear Paul calling to me over it, "They never answer." Ended up, I shouted through their letterbox, *Police!* That got them out, well half out. The brother's wife, or whatever she is, was peeking round the living-room door all the time I was talking to him, telling him about the accident and saying he might, you know, want to stick a couple more quid in the meter and maybe go up there and sit with the fella for a while. I'm not kidding, you'd have thought the way they were looking at me I was the one had driven into him.'

They sat on for another half hour after that, but the mood, in their small corner, had changed. The night's events brought back to mind, and to the conversation, moments when they or those dear to them, or those known to those who were, had experienced scrapes and near misses, and not in traffic accidents either. Tales of flying masonry and shards of glass this size landing inches from heads, bullets lodged in window frames, cupboard doors, a headboard, if you could beat that (no one could); of a dressing table brought home from a furniture store with an unexploded incendiary device in the bottom drawer, an elderly aunt who had an actual heart attack when she went to put away her slips and briefs, and lived to fight and argue and generally be a pain in the BTM another day.

Kurtis Bain's songs were beginning to blend into one another. Diners started drifting out. The Post Office crowd went raucously just before the end of his second set. The applause when he took his final bow was enthusiastic but sparse.

For all that he had been distracted for large chunks of his performance, Herbie didn't want to leave without thanking the kid in person.

He and the girl with the finger curls were sharing a hot chocolate with whipped cream and marshmallows on top, two long spoons crossing in the ever-shrinking space between their mouths.

'That was great,' Herbie said. 'I've got to ask you, but, where did you hear all that stuff?'

Kurtis Bain succeeded in dragging his attention away from his girl. 'My great-granny had these old reel-to-reel tapes, they were mouldering away for years in a box in the roof space, nearly got thrown out when my dad and his brothers were clearing out after she died. The guys who came to pick the skip up had the chains and all hooked on to the sides before I spied them and made a grab.'

'Seriously?'

'Nah.' Kurtis Bain licked cream off his top lip. 'YouTube.' His girl bit down on her spoon, which is to say his. 'I'm just working on my back story.'

Derek arrived – just in time – at Herbie's shoulder. 'Everyone seemed to have a good night anyway,' he said.

Except Paul, Herbie wanted to say, and me for this last quarter of a minute of it, but, yeah, he said instead, it all went over well.

'I must have looked a right fool back there,' Beth said as they walked home. 'A soldier!'

'You're across the water, you're not to know that kind of thing still goes on.'

'That's not entirely true. I had a text a couple of years back from a girl in my class, Janet… Do you remember Janet?' He didn't. 'She had really bad eczema.' It wasn't ringing a bell. 'Oh, you know, her dad was a friend of someone you used to work with…'

'She texted,' Herbie said, rerouting her.

'She did. A guy who used to sit in front of the two of us in RE was done for blowing some wee fella's kneecaps off. I'm talking a married man, couple of kids of his own. I actually used to get on all right with him. I mean, he seemed as keen as the rest of us back then to steer clear of the real scumbags.'

'I hate that word.'

'Hate away, you didn't have to go to school with them. The fights and things there used to be… and some of the other stuff went on. I'm telling you, they should have given us campaign medals at the end of it instead of certificates.'

'You never told us any of this at the time.'

'I never told you anything about anything. You wouldn't

have let me out of the house otherwise. And it wasn't as if there wasn't stuff going on in other schools. They are holding centres for the most emotionally volatile section of the entire population. What do you expect?'

As they were turning into the street Herbie saw Peadar and Norrie come out of their gate at the far end and cut across to the pavement opposite, bent on some new mission.

('Find the fucker who wrecked Paul's car, Norrie. Find the fucker who wrecked Paul's car.')

'Does that dog only have three legs?' Beth asked out the corner of her mouth as the two drew near.

'Yes, but don't let on to it, it doesn't know.'

Peadar saluted. 'Can't stop.' And didn't. Nor did Norrie.

4

Next morning, bright and early, Tanya phoned.
'What's going on?'

'Good morning to you too, Tanya.'

'Beth messaged me last night. She says she's in Belfast…
and she's bankrupt?'

It was hard to say which she was struggling with more.

'Sorry, I should have let you know before now.'

'That stupid giraffe.'

'What?'

'The money box your mum and dad gave her.'

'You've lost me.'

'Oh, come on: her third or fourth birthday.'

'I always thought that was a zebra,' Herbie said. A zebra,
admittedly, designed by somebody who had never seen
so much as a picture of one and had had it described by
somebody who had never seen a zebra either.

'It was stupid whatever it was. Martin says you should never
give a child a piggy bank.'

'Or giraffey.'

'Don't be funny. They never learn how to budget, they just hoard and splurge, hoard and splurge.'

'She did all right up to now.' He couldn't quite understand how he had ended up acting for their daughter's defence. Or maybe it was himself he was defending – him and Tanya both, together. *We didn't make a* complete *mess of things.* A saying of his aunt June's swam up from the depths. 'Yous will know better with the next one.' He pushed it down again with the same distaste as he had back then. 'Anyway,' he told Tanya, 'you only have to turn on the news, bankruptcies have been running at record levels all over.'

'Not the Crash again! I thought we were supposed to be over that.'

'It's like just when everyone else at school is starting to get better, your child goes and gets whatever it was that was doing the rounds.'

Even before the sentence was fully out, he was transported back to the bathroom in Oriel, all yellows and blues and ornamental starfish. Beth kneeling on the floor, her head over the edge of the bath, sobbing, while he made lines in her hair with the pointed handle of a plastic comb on the hunt, sector by sector, follicle by follicle if need be, for nits. 'The other girls are all saying they caught them from me…'

'I still don't know why she came to you,' Tanya said.

'Thanks.'

Tanya carried on over it. 'She always found it easier to talk to me.'

'Maybe it's part of her bankruptcy conditions that she has to stay in the UK.'

'I hadn't thought of that.' Tanya instantly sounded cheerier. 'That's probably what it is right enough. As long as she gets out before they call a Border Poll.'

'I think she's safe a while yet.'

'I wouldn't be so sure: the way things are going Up There. Even Down Here people who would never have given the Shinners the time of day are starting to say, Do you know what...?'

Up There, Down Here. Tanya's Ireland in a nutshell.

She and Martin had met at a yoga retreat in Omeath, a few miles into the Irish Republic, and had moved steadily southwards, holing up for a bit, while separations were formalised, in a flat in Temple Bar (Martin's maternal grandmother had grown up in it, though it was a whole different Temple Bar then, a whole different Dublin), moving on to Kilkenny for a couple of years, followed by three more in Kanturk, before taking up residence in a farmhouse on the outskirts of Schull, about fifteen miles short of the Mizen Head, from where it was pretty much next stop Cape Cod.

It encouraged you, Tanya said, to take the long view.

'Tell me you still have your Irish passport.'

Passports – the need to hold more than one at a time – had always been a particular obsession of Tanya's.

'It's expired. I have the renewal application in the kitchen drawer.'

'I'd fill it in today if I was you and get it sent away. Martin says you might want to look at opening a bank account Down Here too. There'll be currency controls next.'

'How is Martin?' Well, if Herbie was going to be treated to the gospel according to him…

'He's lying here beside me if you want to say hello.'

Herbie thought he heard a light slap. Bare arse. A grunt. He saw it all: the rumpled bed, the light-walled room, the curtains open on to fields, glimpses of the Atlantic beyond.

'No,' he said, 'don't disturb him.'

Actually, he hadn't been completely straight with Tanya about the passport application form. It *had* been in the kitchen drawer (not, obviously, the kitchen drawer Tanya would have remembered, his-and-hers, though the function was the same), from way before the Referendum was even called. And he *had* thought in the days after the result that it mightn't be a bad idea to get it in. Then he heard from Neeta that there had been such a rush of applications from north of the border and from people across the water whose great-grandparents had once spent a weekend in Galway that they had run out of passports in Dublin, and not wanting to look as though he was part of the general panic (the image in his mind was of helicopters taking off from embassy rooftops) he decided to hold off a while longer. And then other stuff went into the kitchen drawer. And then other stuff on top of that. When he did take the form out again he realised it had been signed and witnessed exactly three years previously. The notes said the photographs couldn't be more than six months old. He tore the whole lot up. He would pick up another form. Soon.

Beth came downstairs, still a touch bleary.

'I've had your mum on the phone,' he said.

She yawned. 'I texted her last night.'

'She told me. She's a bit put out you didn't do it sooner.'

That woke her. 'This would be the same woman who notified me of her last change of address with a pre-printed postcard.'

'I got one of those too.'

'I don't want to be harsh here, Dad, but she fell out of love with you. I'm her daughter. A little bit of forewarning would have been nice.'

'From what I can gather it all happened very quickly.' An elderly uncle of Martin's, on his father's side, last of three unmarried brothers, taken into a home.

'Funny,' she said.

'What is?'

'I used to take such comfort when I was small – nights I was lying tucked up in bed, or sitting in the back of the car listening to you and Mum talking in the front – thinking that we were this perfect unit, one of everything: mother, father, child… little heteronormative creature that I was. I couldn't imagine any of it changing, ever – and now look at us, literally all over the place.'

'You know you can stay here for as long as you need to.'

'That wasn't what I meant.'

'OK, but you can just the same.'

She nodded. 'Excuse me,' she said, and went into the bathroom. Came out again a minute or two later. 'Another couple of weeks would be a help.'

A couple of weeks passed, became a few.

They met in the kitchen again one morning as he was making himself a sandwich to take to work.

'I've been thinking,' she said. 'It's not right. I can't just be living here and not contributing.'

'Nonsense. It's as easy and cheap to cook for two as one. Need I mention the lee—'

She held up her hand: no more leeks, even in jest. 'All right, but I was thinking I should look for some work.'

'Can you work?'

'Of course I can. The sooner the better, in fact.'

'But then is it not up to the receiver to decide what you can and can't do with your money?'

'She'll be fine with me paying you housekeeping.'

'She?'

'What's the matter, not think a woman's up to the job?

'I just had never thought of it as an actual person.'

'An actual person with an actual name. Polly. She's lovely. Messages me a couple of times a week to see how I'm getting on. Fond of her emojis. Even has one for you. Where is it…?' She dragged out her phone from her jeans pocket, performed a couple of quick swipes – 'Ah!' She showed him a face, careful to cover the rest of the message with her thumb: thick yellow moustache, tufts of yellow hair either side of a bald yellow head.

'That's me?'

'I don't know.' She held the phone up, tilting the screen a little to the left and then to the right. 'In a certain light…'

'I can ask around, if you like.'

'I was thinking I would make up some cards, call in a few places, see if they're looking for anyone.'

He left her sitting at the table with her water and lemon slice and his laptop, playing around with fonts and text effects.

She was sitting there when he came home at four, a small stack of cards by her elbow: *work wanted, anything considered,* which wouldn't have been quite the wording he would have suggested.

'You haven't been at that all day, have you?'

'Are you kidding? I must have walked the whole of east Belfast. I was going to phone someone: I think I spotted a street that doesn't have a Cash 4 Clothes shop on it yet.'

'You're not going to try and tell me it's any different across the water.'

'God, no, but when you look at all the money coming in here, those big new hotels down the town, they're not exactly spreading the love, are they? Maybe if a few of those people getting their photos taken at the murals walked a couple of hundred feet and spent a few quid instead of getting back in their buses and their black taxis.'

'I'm sorry if it was a wasted day.'

'I wouldn't say wasted.' She searched for something in the shoulder bag hanging from the back of her chair. 'See, I picked this up.' She had pulled out an A5 flier in the local football team's colours: pre-season friendly, the Saturday after next. Another search produced the ticket from the raffle at Sam's. 'You shall go to the football, Cinders!'

'Me?'

'Well, you have been so good letting me stay all this time...'

'I'm your father.'

'Yeah, but even so, if anybody deserves that ticket' – she pushed it across the table towards him as she spoke – 'it's you.'

He pushed it back. 'It was you won the raffle.'

'I know, but' – back to him – 'take it.'

'I wouldn't want' – to her – 'to deprive you.'

'For the love of God. Please.' Slumped across the table, arms outstretched, knuckles whitening as she held the ticket in both hands. 'I'm begging you. Take it.'

Herbie had walked past the football ground every other day since he had moved here, with hardly a second glance.

With its rendered concrete wall, corrugated-iron fences and enormous wooden gates, it was a throwback to another era, of rattles and bobble hats and alternating coloured scarves, that was already old when he was a boy. His father had taken him along to a few Home Internationals at Windsor Park while Herbie was still in primary school, although about the only things that stuck in his head, beyond the assault on the senses that was the men's toilets (were there any other kind then?), were the crush on the railway bridge leading to the ground and his father's disappointment that, once the match had kicked off, all Herbie wanted to know was how long it was to half time and if they were going to get a hot dog. What little interest he had had in the game then, the intervening years of crazy wages and blanket coverage had more or less completely put paid to.

Still, for all her overacting, Beth had given him the ticket. He could always stick his head in for half an hour, just to tell her he had been.

So it was, at five minutes to the hour appointed, on the Saturday after the Saturday after, he handed over the golden ticket at the turnstile, wondering if he had ever actually walked through one on his own, the convention in his primary-school days being that boys under a certain age could be handed up over the turnstile, free, by the adult who had brought them, or – in the case of boys who had turned up on spec – by any other adult whose eye and ear they could catch. 'Mister, mister, lift us over…'

The man operating the turnstile this afternoon, clocking Herbie's ticket, asked him his name and squeezed his fingers through the gap in the glass for something like a shake before admitting him to a lopsided stadium – if that was the word: crumbling terraces to the left, a blank-faced redbrick pavilion or possibly social club beyond, and, to the right, across a low ditch, a grass bank rising steeply to the perimeter wall. It lacked only the watchtower to tell you all thoughts of escape were futile. The pitch in between, though, was unexpectedly lush and green in a way Herbie had not seen since his first time looking at a colour TV screen. Someone had invested an awful lot of time, and pride, in its preparation.

Herbie was looking about for a place to stand, preferably with a bit of shelter (the day again slow to declare), when he heard a voice – the man who had taken his ticket, he would almost have sworn – over the Tannoy... *Big welcome... Prize-winner... Herbie Murray...* The couple of dozen men and three women distributed about the terraces applauded.

Another voice, from close to one of the corner flags and channelled by cupped hands, sang, 'Herbie, Herbie, give us a wave... Herbie, give us a wave,' which he did eventually, after a fashion, fingers fluttering, like he was owning up to a fart, and the applause rose again.

There was no way now he was going to be able to slip away unnoticed.

A few moments later the teams ran down the steps of the pavilion-cum-social club and on to the pitch. A couple of the players – he couldn't tell which team was which at first – looked as though they wouldn't make it to the end of the warm-up, with its sprints and turns and stretches, never mind to the end of the match, but then the referee called them all to order and the captains shook hands and – one trill on the referee's whistle – the match kicked off... and Holy God, Herbie felt as though he had been thumped in the chest. The players were close enough that he could hear the thud of their boots on the turf as they passed in front of him at speeds he would never from the warm-up have imagined they had in them. He could hear their calls – *use me, use me, use me* – and even their comments to one another – *I was shouting to you to use me* – when the play had moved to a more distant part of the pitch. He could hear their laboured breathing. And as for the tackles... *Ooof!*

'Referee! He's a fucking hallion!' the taller of the men two steps back and slightly to the right of Herbie nearly lifted off the ground as he shouted after one particularly brutal-looking takedown. From various comments his mate made in the course of the next few minutes (because the commentary, like the play, was unrelenting), Herbie worked out that this tall man was the father of the player who had been tackled – one of the home team – not that that stopped the same player getting stick from other quarters.

'Take your boots off and give them up here to your da, wee man... Tell that eejit beside you to do the same.' ('Ah, now, Davy's da's in the hospital.' 'Sure, I know, and he couldn't do any worse.')

The boots all the while continued to thud as the ball – seemingly outside of anyone's control for more than a second or two at a time – moved from one end of the lush grass to the other without once troubling either goal.

One end to the other, one end to the other, one end to the other.

And then like that the referee was trilling on his whistle again and it was half time.

A bearded man three steps in front of Herbie turned.

'Well, be honest, what did you think?'

But before he could answer the man's mate chipped in, 'The best thing you could say about that is nobody's eye is out.'

'There's still forty-five minutes,' the bearded man said ominously.

A couple of people appeared at the door of the redbrick building, pints in their hands. Herbie went in and ordered a half, thinking only of the time available, and was given a pint regardless, with no money accepted in return. 'We'll call that a bonus prize,' the barman said.

A large screen in the corner was showing a match from somewhere where the crowd was bigger and the grass less green. A player appeared in close-up. It was like looking through a keyhole. Where was everybody else?

Sound of studs on tiles. Smell of wintergreen rub. The teams were coming back out. Herbie tipped his head back and swallowed. And again... and again, until finally he had seen the pint off.

Midway through the second half – which until that moment had been as formless as the first – one of the away team's wide men cut inside from the far touchline, dragging the ball this way and that with the bottom of his right boot, trying to make an opening, then just when it looked as though the three men in front of him had shut him out – when he seemed himself to have abandoned all hope of finding a way through – he flipped the ball up with the toe of his left and with the same foot walloped a shot that came off a post (nearly broke it in two), off the other post and into the net.

Even he looked stunned, slowly raising his arms, palms upturned. Jesus Christ.

Only the goal didn't stand: the referee gestured with both hands – a push on a defender by one of the wide man's teammates inside the box. 'Aw, come on, Ref,' said the player the teammate was adjudged to have pushed, 'it's a friendly, give him the goal.'

'Do, Ref,' the wide man said. 'When I am ever going to do something like that again?' He turned to the terraces. 'Did any of yous have your phones out there?'

'Sure, it looked like you were running away from the goal,' the tall man behind Herbie called.

'Typical. I bet you if I'd fallen on my frigging arse yous would have it all over Instagram before I'd even got to my feet again.'

He complained so much in the end the referee showed him a yellow card and ten minutes later showed him another – although the consensus was it was a straight red – for going into a tackle with his studs up.

He protested all the way off the pitch: 'Swear to God, I was trying to pull out.'

'That's what your da said to your ma when they had you,' came the answering shout from the terraces. And so it went on. Less Theatre of Dreams than music hall. The match finished – the remaining twenty-one players on the field embracing, spent – scoreless, which felt about right.

Herbie imagined people beyond the rendered concrete wall asking him how it went and rolling their eyes at the 'nil–nil' with no idea of all that the players and spectators alike had gone through to arrive at it.

The bearded man in front of him pumped his hand in parting. 'That's you now,' he said, 'inducted into the cult. You'll curse the day you ever won that raffle.'

And the best, or the worst, of it was, it wasn't even him that won.

His guard must have been down (replaying the goal that never was: even the second post shook) or the pint was belatedly kicking in. He found himself, a quarter of an hour later, standing at the till in M&S Simply Food facing Brian.

Whose eyes lit up.

'Here, what about this one: man goes to the doctor. Doctor, he says, I keep hearing voices. Doctor says it's not a doctor you need, it's a psychiatrist, but your man says no, doctor, they're coming from my leg. Your *leg*…? Doctor's saying to himself, this fella's worse than I thought, but then – humour him – he listens a moment…'

'Brian' – the patter had brought Herbie to his senses – 'you do know there's a queue behind me?'

'That's all right, they'll all wait, won't you?' he said and, before any of the four of them could reply, 'Doctor listens and right enough he can hear this tiny wee voice from somewhere, so he takes his stethoscope out, puts it to your man's thigh and the wee voice says, "Lend us a tenner," clear as a bell. That's strange. He moves the stethoscope down to the fella's knee, there it is again, "Lend us a tenner," down to his shin, "Lend us a tenner." Doctor straightens up, frowning. He says, I'm sorry to have to tell you, your leg's broke in three places.'

The lanky boy three back in the queue laughed.

'Did you like that one?' Brian said, past Herbie, who took the opportunity to pocket his change and beat it out the... *Oof! Referee!* A woman was coming in the door, at speed, as he was going out. His hands shot out towards her shoulders as her hands – *her* hands – went up as a buffer against his chest. For a moment they were looking into one another's eyes. He knew from her expression she recognised him too.

'Sorry, sorry, sorry.' (Both of them together.)

'I was rushing.' (Just her.) 'Late for my shift.'

'That's a better' (him) 'excuse than mine.' They took their hands back, their fingers in withdrawing making small unconscious adjustments to one another's sleeves and shirtfronts. 'You sure you're OK?'

'I'll be sitting on my behind for the next four hours. That might just have been the jolt I needed to keep me from nodding off.'

He could sense even as the words were forming that he might be about to embarrass himself, but it was too late to stop. 'Well, if ever I can help by slamming into you again, I'm just around the corner.'

She looked at him, eyes narrowing... (and, lo, was the man who said he would curse the day about to be proved right... oh, wait...) no, not narrowing, *creasing*: that was a smile of sorts. 'I'll keep that in mind.'

'Good. I mean, do. I mean, right.'

'Right.'

It had been a bit of a while since he had had cause to speculate, but he was pretty sure something had just happened. Even assuming it had, though, there was absolutely no reason to suppose that there was the slightest possibility or expectation of anything more.

What was Tanya's term? Mini-flirts? Entirely without consequence. (And in fairness to Tanya they had played no part in her separation from him.) 'Just a wee recharging of the self-esteem batteries.' Zap. That was nice. Now move on.

He managed to stay away a week, well, a working week, well, nearly all of it anyway. Thursday night he stopped by a couple of minutes before closing to see what bread had been reduced.

It was pure chance that her till was free. She didn't look at all surprised to see him and his 50p sourdough.

'So, your name's Herbie… Brian told me… And I probably shouldn't have asked, and he probably shouldn't have said, but your buying habits strongly suggest a man shopping for one… most of the time…'

'Daughter's staying for a while,' he said.

She nodded. 'And despite your dubious lines about slamming into people you actually seem quite nice, and sane.' She whispered behind her hand. 'This is the part you pay me.' All his fingers of a sudden thumbs. He held out a palm full of coins from which she selected a twenty and three tens. 'If you wanted to do something some time, I would not be averse to that,' she said and smiled. 'Don't forget your receipt.'

'I'm all right without it.'

'Go on,' she held it out, folded, between two fingers, which she twitched, 'take the receipt.'

It felt like contraband in his trouser pocket – past the four remaining tills he smuggled it, past the security guard, who might, he thought now, have been there to guard against precisely this sort of carry-on, across the car park, the lights just beginning to pink against the navy-blue sky, past, or rather between, a couple of short-shirt-sleeved officers of the Police Service of Northern Ireland, stepping aside and saying, 'Right?' in that tone that seemed to anticipate the exact opposite... He didn't take the receipt out until he was well down his own street. The ridiculous sensation even five hundred yards from the supermarket door that he was being watched. She had folded another slip of paper inside it with a mobile number on it in purple pen. No name, no need, he had known it from the start.

5

Herbie, or the person who had been using his name, had taken the train, the summer of the year he turned seventeen, down the Rhine Valley. Him and the girl who he had been going out with since the summer before, and who he had seriously begun to think – because those were the times and those the mores – he might one of these days propose to. There was a photo in one of the evidence boxes, the two of them standing at the station on York Road with their rucksacks, wide of smile and trouser leg, waiting for the two-carriage boneshaker that would dump them three quarters of an hour later, smiles only just intact, at the Larne–Stranraer ferry terminal. Twenty-four hours after that again (after sex on the deck of the night ferry – mad – and in the toilets of the Stranraer-to-Euston train – stinking – and again on the ferry, entirely unnoticed in broad daylight – ship's rail, rear-fastening skirt – ingenious) they were squeezed up against the window of the SNCF, France already far behind them, staring out at hilltop Schlosses: 'I'd have that one...' 'Nah, that one over the river there...' 'I'll flash a light from mine to yours, ready when you are…' 'Like the boxes of Daz.' 'Daz?' 'In the living-room window… women in Craigavon… to let their fancy men know the coast was clear.' 'That's OMO: Old Man Out.' 'No?' 'Yes.' 'Hold on, my mum's just switched to OMO.'

Alice, you called her, Alice Clark, which amused the Germans they met no end. '*Alice Clark*,' they said and laughed. 'I don't understand,' she said, 'what's so funny?'

'*Alles klar, alles klar*: "everything is fine".'

They got off the train the second day at a place called Treis-Karden for no other reason than they liked the look of the station. Their introduction to Rhine wine (to wine of any origin for her) and in pretty short order to being sick on Rhine wine. Oh, Christ, were they sick, in tandem and in turn. They slept outside the first couple of nights, not even bothering to pitch a tent, then got jobs in a restaurant on the river's edge, clearing tables, washing dishes and salting away unfinished bottles of wine. (They had only got sick that first night, not completely sickened.) It paid buttons, but there was a room thrown in with two single beds that they wasted no time in pushing together under the window. At nights when really and truly they could fuck no more they knelt on the mattress, passing a bottle of leftover wine between them, watching the enormous Rhine barges passing silently with their cargoes of coal in this direction, of timber in that.

'It's not that hard being happy, is it?' she said.

And he said, '*Alles klar*, Alice Clark, *alles klar*.'

Three weeks went by. Then, as abruptly as they had arrived, they packed their rucksacks again and got back on the train, headed down through Saarland. She sang in his ear, 'this land is Saarland, this land was made for you and me', her own bilingual gag. At Saarbrücken ('over bridge of Saars, to rest my eyes in shades of green') they kissed goodbye... for now. She was going on to Switzerland to see a girl she knew from Guides. (That she herself had been a Guide – was still – only added to the delight that they both took in their Rhine-bank bacchanal.) She was to write as soon as she got there with the arrangements for meeting up the following weekend – Kehl, they thought, and from there to Strasbourg – but the letter when it came was a Dear Herbie. She hadn't intended it, not for a minute, but she had met this amazing guy – 'he got on the train in Saarbrücken as you were getting off, came all the way down the carriage and stopped right beside me, wanted to know if the seat was taken'. (*Did I walk past him on the platform, in the aisle, even?* He ran through the suspects in his mind. He thought he was probably looking for a guy with a wispy beard, beat-up guitar slung across his back, coloured string for a strap.) 'I mean,' she ended, 'what are the chances of that?'

He had been writing her a letter with all the things she had missed out on – the Mithraic cave temple that frankly would have been an open invitation to them if they had gone in there together. This land *was* Saarland now, but it had been many things besides in recent centuries, slipping this way and that over the French border, or the border slipping this way and

89

that about it, making Northern Ireland look like a model of stability and easily parsed identity. He had taken a photograph of the bronze hand coming out of the wall of an old church, just off the main road from the train station, a twist of bronze rope connecting it to another hand further down. Just some ancient craftsman's idea of a joke, he had thought – handrail, get it? – until, bending, he read the inscription, in French, on one of the hands: *à mon seul desir*… and his heart flipped.

He tore the letter up. *Alles* fucking *klar*.

He decided not to hang around there but caught the train the very next day, back up the valley, back through Treis-Karden – there went the restaurant with the window from which they had watched the Rhine barges, there went the his-and-hers Schlosses – all the way – at last, at last – to Calais. Almost the first person he saw when he arrived at the ferry terminal was a girl his own age sitting on her hunkers in front of a bright blue rucksack building a tower of coins, one centime at a time. Twice he watched the tower fall and rise again before he went over and asked if she could do with a hand. She told him as they worked, centime about, that she had had her passport and all her money nicked in a hostel in Paris (two words into her story he knew she was from Belfast too): a pair of American 'sisters' she had taken pity on in the street outside, the two of them acting all like, oh, this is our first ever time in Europe, and, oh, we don't even know what anyone is saying to us, and, oh, maybe the three of us could, you know, share… The smiles on them when she said, sure, why not!

The cops told her later they had been working this con for a couple of years at hostels up and down the country. The elder one was actually in her thirties. The cops were working on the theory she was the younger one's mother. I mean, how creepy was that?'

The British embassy had given her a temporary passport – it looked like something from a war movie, the kind of thing you'd be sweating over when the German guards took it off you for inspection – and twenty francs, of which she had already spent – she ran her fingers up the pile of coins – seventeen francs and thirty-six centimes. He pulled out the last ten francs he had to his name and bought her a coffee and a baguette with cheese hanging out the end of it, and in between slurping the one and horsing into the other she told him about her boyfriend who had chickened out of travelling with her the day before they were due to leave home. 'Here he was to me, "you never know what could happen over there..." I know what wouldn't have happened if he hadn't been such a lapper and come with me, I would never have started talking to those American bitches in the first place.'

Two conclusions she had reached: never trust a perfect smile and always carry a second passport. 'Yous tell me I'm Irish as well as British? Fair enough, give me the passport, then. There has to be some advantage to living in that crummy country of ours.'

They talked the whole way back – across the Channel, up through England, Scotland, across the water again – to Larne where the boneshaker had left him less than a month before and where her brother was waiting at the terminal doors to pick her up in his bread van, Ormo it said on the side. (OMO boxes and lights flashing across the Rhine Valley already felt like another lifetime.) She placed a kiss chastely on his cheek. 'Wait, how am I going to find you again?' he asked, and she took hold of his wrist and wrote her number up his forearm – there – and signed it Tanya, with a little smiling flower of a full stop.

I mean, what were the chances?

He waited another two days before he rang Louise. 'I knew you wouldn't call yesterday,' she said. 'It's like, nobody orders the first bottle of wine on the menu any more. They probably don't even bother keeping the first bottle on the racks.'

'I once phoned a girl from the phone box round the corner from her house,' he said, 'about a minute and a half after she gave me her number. Here she was, "Is that you, Herbie?" I said to her, "You surprised to hear from me so soon?" She said, "If you're phoning from where I think you're phoning from, I'm surprised you could even bear to step inside." And swear to God it was only as she was saying that that the smell hit me, I'd been so puppy-dog keen to call her it was like all my other senses were suspended, and I looked down at the ground and...'

'Stop,' she said. 'I get the picture. I take it all back, you were right not to rush in.'

He suggested a film, or a play. 'I was thinking more of the two of us talking,' she said, 'rather than paying to listen to other people. Music's OK, but not too much. Drink should definitely be involved.'

'Hm, I'm beginning to see the outline of the sort of establishment you have in mind.'

'Can you see bras hanging from the ceiling?'

'I can now.'

'Right, then, we're flying. How is Tuesday night for you?'

'A rare blank in an otherwise jam-packed calendar.'

'We will grab it while we can then.'

He told Beth he was going out to meet a friend. It sounded unnatural even to his own ears.

'Sam's opening on Tuesdays as well as Thursdays now?'

'Not Sam's. In town.'

'This is a bit of a departure,' she said. 'Tell me if it's none of my business, but anyone I know?'

'Her name's Louise.'

She did the arched eyebrows thing at mention of 'her'.

'She works round in the M&S.'

'First time meeting in the real world?'

He nodded.

'She's very lucky,' she said, no trace now of tease. 'And you look very smart, without looking like you were too worried about it.'

Which was nice of her, though entirely wrong. Because he had been worried, almost from the moment he had put down the phone to Louise. Who knew that two jackets, five shirts and three sweaters could throw up so many combinations? Though it was probably an immutable law that no matter how many there were you would revert in the end to the first one you tried.

The place with the bras on the ceiling (they were not so much hanging from as strung across, like bunting) was famous for… the bras on the ceiling, obviously, but also for occupying the site of what had once been Belfast's smallest bar. Mind you, how it managed to be both on the site of and twice the size of was a feat no one had yet been able to explain to Herbie. He had been in it once when it was still the smallest bar. Another customer – *the* other customer – was talking to the barman about the bad old days of pub bombings and shootings.

'You were lucky to come through it, all the same.'

'Well, a fella did try to leave a bomb in here one night,' the barman said, 'but there was no room. Now, duck down there while I serve that man behind you.'

The present-day bouncers, one woman, one man, each flanked by a storage heater (first sign of the season changing), nodded as Herbie crossed the short forecourt and pushed open the door. Noise – beards – aroma of botanicals – air of immortality: how could this ever end, any of it?

He had been inside two minutes before he realised Louise was already there ahead of him, in a corner at the back of the room, beneath a wall-length frieze of glass display cases featuring hats and veils and mannequin heads. A little more austerely dressed than he had imagined, gold and blue patterned scarf, black pearl earrings.

She lifted her bag from the seat to make room for him. 'I always make a beeline for this corner.'

'You're a regular?'

'I drop in for a drink the odd time when I'm in town. I thought at least if you didn't come the bar staff would be used to seeing me on my own.'

'Why would I not have come?'

'I don't know. You could have been hit by a bus. It's a rare occurrence, but pianos have been known to drop.'

He dragged a hand across his forehead. 'I feel like I've had a narrow escape.'

'Celebrate every day, I say.'

'In that case, what will you have to drink?'

'Surprise me.'

'I was hoping you wouldn't say that.'

'Cocktail of the day, then.'

He battled through to the bar and ordered two. No liquid darker than water in the mix, though honeycomb was also enlisted, the hard kind he was brought up to call Yellow Man. She asked him as soon as he came back with the drinks – held high above his head – about his marriage.

'Might as well get it out of the way… Leaver or left?'

He could have asked her why she presumed he had been married, but let's face it, she had presumed right. 'Left.'

'Relieved or bereft?'

'Somewhere in between.'

'We'll call that rereft. Long ago?'

He blew his cheeks out. 'Some days it feels like another lifetime.'

'And have you done much of this sort of thing since?'

'Let me see, this must be the…' Counting on his fingers, left hand, right hand, left hand, right hand, then back to the left again, stopping at the index finger, 'first. And what about you?'

'See when you were doing the actual adding up on your fingers there? That, and then some.'

'I actually meant your marriage. Who did the leaving there?'

She took a moment, tilted her glass. Clack, went the Yellow Man. 'I would have left him, but…'

'There's always a but,' he was about to say and was instantly glad he didn't.

'… but the cops got to him first.' She turned the glass on its mat a couple of times. Clack, clack, clack. 'Indecent images,' she said. 'Thousands and thousands of them. His hard drive was like a warehouse where other creeps like him came to browse and buy. He was some sort of celebrity in those circles. I had no idea, I mean none whatsoever, but nobody believes you. If it had been some other woman in my position I probably wouldn't have believed her: seriously, I'd have been, how could you spend all that time with someone and not know? But it was me, and, I swear, I didn't. I got so tired of having to say it I was nearly going to get cards printed and deliver them door to door, but it was less of a heartache in the end just to sell up and move to another part of town.'

'So, you did leave, sort of.'

'I'd have been better off leaving the country altogether. I still see people the odd time, from where I used to be, they'll come into the store, half an hour to kill before a big concert down the road in the Odyssey' (this didn't seem the moment to remind her that the arena in question had sloughed off the O, the d and both the ys), 'and it's all, ah, Louise, how are you keeping, haven't seen you for an age, but they can't get away fast enough. You'd think I had a contagion.'

'That first time I met you,' he said, 'I was embarrassed for days afterwards.'

'You stared.'

'I did and I'd have been even more embarrassed if I had known all that. You were probably thinking to yourself, oh brilliant, here's another one come to stand and gawp.'

'No, gawping's different. Your sort of staring stopped annoying me a long time ago.' Then, 'Wait,' she said, to herself as it sounded, 'that came out wrong. It's just. People have this reaction, women as well as men, they think they recognise me but they've no idea how.'

She had turned as she said this until she was looking him straight in the face or rather letting him look at her, her features composed as though for a game of charades. She held her hands up in front of her face, fingers spread. Ten letters? Ten syllables? Ten words?

'I'm sorry...'

'Billboards?' she said.

Add a little sparkle to her Christmas with a diamond from... 'You're not a hand model, are you?'

She let both hands drop into her lap, palms up.

'Have you been watching *Zoolander*?' He looked at her blankly. She shook her head – never mind – raised her hands

97

again, spoke out from behind them. 'The fingers are supposed to represent prison bars. *Don't be locked in by despair...*'

'*Call the Samaritans today...* Oh, God, yeah, I remember now. That was you?'

'Yes.'

'But those used to be everywhere. Them and the confidential telephone number... and... and that was about it. You and the RUC, you had the market cornered.'

'I know. But you couldn't really see it was me, that was the point of the ad.'

And right enough, when he tried now to call it to mind, he still couldn't have said what colour her hair was.

'And were you, then?'

'Locked in by despair? A Samaritan? I was married to the photographer.'

'You mean... Oh.'

'Sorry, I left that bit out. Lots of those images the cops found, that warehouse he had built up, he took them himself.' She looked him straight in the face again. 'It crossed your mind there too, didn't it? "Really and truly, how could she not know?"'

'That wasn't what I was thinking at all.'

She held his gaze a moment or two longer then took a drink. Moving on. 'I didn't just work with him. I did other bits and pieces. I nearly had a national campaign once, a magazine ad for brandy. I went over to London to do the shoot and of course there was fake snow everywhere and a massive great St Bernard that kept wanting to stick its bloody tongue in my ear, up my sleeve, anywhere it spied an inch of bare flesh, which in those days as you can probably imagine was pretty much every-where. Ended up I grabbed hold of one of its ears and said, listen, Buster, any more of that you're getting this bottle right over your head.'

'You're just right.'

'I don't know if I was. The ad agency people had me into my own clothes and in a taxi back to Heathrow before you could say... think of something dog-related.'

'Woof?'

'Woof? You missed your calling. Anyway, apparently the female humans were interchangeable. The dog was the star. The bloody St Bernard.'

From where it was a very short step indeed to Herbie's telling her about Norrie, and about how he had taken rescue dog the wrong way the first time Peadar had said it. She agreed with Peadar, he was, in fairness, a bit of a dope. For a while after that, all the same, they swapped scenarios – supermarket shoppers dragged by their collars from beneath avalanches of two-for-one extra-soft toilet rolls; pairs of shoes, laced together, liberated from the telegraph wires where they had been dangling for decades: the grace of Norrie as he glided along, Great Blondin style, on his one firm back paw...

There was a break then for a replenishing of glasses, on the far side of which Louise crossed the species divide and started telling him about the cat sanctuary where she had worked one summer between O Levels and A Levels – not much more than a big shed out the back of some woman's house, half a dozen rows of cages stacked two or three high, with these cats people had handed in, kittens most of them, often entire litters at a time, or the odd boy cat that turned out to be a girl.

The woman had started with a stray that turned up on her back step looking to be fed and it had just kept growing from there. Of course, it couldn't just go on and on expanding, there needed to be cats going out as well as coming in. She had like an open day, every couple of Saturdays, and there'd always be a few would get adopted, but nowhere like enough. The hardest of all to find homes for – no surprise – were the older ones, family pets whose owners had died or grown too frail to care for them. The woman who ran the place had the idea of attaching little slate boards next to the cage doors with their occupants' names and ages and a little about their background and temperament – 'quite a shy cat', 'a very comfortable cat around children', 'fond of having his tummy tickled' – humanising is not the word, but you know, giving them a personality. And it worked. People started *talking* to them, through the bars of their cages – 'So you like snooker on the telly, do you? Well me too' – and then the next thing they would be wanting to take them out and stroke them, by which time, of course, the deal was sealed.

There was this one, but, Louise said, right at the end of a row, third cage up, big tabby, just sat there all day every day hunched up, the way they do, staring out. And do you know what was on his board? 'Mike, a...' then a whole big swirl of rubbed-out stuff – you know the way they used to do in the

Beano or the *Dandy* when there was a fight? Like that, and then underneath it, 'cat'. Because whatever you wrote about him he would only go and make a lie of it. So, Mike, a… cat: that's what he was.

'There's something noble in that, all the same,' Herbie said.

'Noble?' Louise shook her head. 'No, not Mike: a cat, like the board said, nothing more.'

'Tell me there's a happy ending at least, somebody comes in looking for a cat, nothing more.'

'I don't know. I went back to school at the end of the summer with the intention of keeping up my Saturday mornings there, but I didn't last more than a couple of weeks. Last I saw of Mike he was sitting in his cage exactly like he always sat. He was like a lifer: the entire rest of the population had changed since I started there. Actually that was the autumn I met *him*.' The now ex-husband, former photographer, current convicted sex offender, she meant. 'I'd no time or thought for anything else, not even my schoolwork in the end, which is partly why I ended up being a lollipop for a St Bernard. It was all, sure why would you want to go away to university? Sure we can have as good a life here the two of us.' She picked up her glass, brought it to just short of her mouth, stopped. 'Baz,' she said flatly, 'a cunt.'

The bar had grown loud around them, the spill from the conversations to the right and the left of them too great to compete with. They finished their drinks and put on their coats and went on to somewhere nearby, quieter, less of what you might call bravura, more of what you would call red leather club chairs. Which they eschewed, ordering a drink instead sitting up at the bar.

'I don't think we should sleep together tonight,' she said when they were getting to the end of it. (A barman glanced up from wiping glasses. Dipped his head a little lower as he resumed lest they should see him smirking.) 'I mean I'm assuming it had crossed your mind too.'

Crossed it to the extent that he had – God help him – checked the use-by on the condoms in the drawer next to his bed, one of which, with six good months still left to it, was in the wallet in his hip pocket.

'I wasn't ruling it out entirely, no.'

'Let's give it one more night.'

'All right.'

He had ended up paying for the odd round in three, so she insisted on booking them each a cab, paid for – appracadabra! – before he even had time to argue.

'So of the several handfuls of nights like that you've had,' he said and got no further. She put her arms up, linking her hands at the back of his head.

'Surprisingly few of them even got as far as this,' she said and kissed him and he had truly truly forgotten how that felt, to lose yourself so utterly, become mere mouth. Mouths.

A phone beeped. One became two again. 'That'll be our taxis,' she said. She turned her head to check, arms still about his neck, then turned again, head bowed, laughing into his chest.

The taxi drivers sat at their wheels, scowling, disapproving parents waiting for their teenage children.

'And that's you probably grounded,' he said.

She left another kiss on his lips and ran.

The reason for his own driver's scowl became more apparent the second Herbie got into the car beside him. His seat resembled nothing so much as an orthopaedic bed in the upright position, headrest doubling as neck brace. There was even a sports drink bottle fitted into a bracket on the door jamb by his right ear, a metal straw coming from it that he could drink from with just a quarter turn of his head. Herbie asked the obvious question (it was a taxi after all, the home of the obvious question): 'Bad back?'

The taxi driver grimaced, addressing his answer to the wing mirror, as he found reverse then first gear. 'Bad back, bad hip, bad knee, can't feel my toes, as my oul lad used to say, I need rubbed out and redrew.'

'I suppose sitting in the car all day…'

The taxi driver turned his martyr's eyes on Herbie's. 'Murder picture. You'd want your head examined doing the like of this week in week out.'

Herbie thought better of the next obvious question, but the driver answered it anyway, pulling down the sun visor, into which was tucked a photograph. He pulled out an inch or two.

'See that there?' he said. A steeply sloping field, scrubby

grass and boulders. 'That's the only reason I put up with all of this. Mine, all the way down to – it's hard to make it out on this – the wee river at the end here.' Two taps of the forefinger. He pushed the photograph back and flipped the visor up again. 'Best part of an acre. I'm going to build a bungalow on it, right at the top. The views in the other direction are nothing ordinary: lake, mountains, forests, the whole shebang. I'm putting floor-to-ceiling glass in all the way round.'

'Would it not make it hard to heat, all that glass?' You could only let so many obvious questions go by.

'It's a special type,' the taxi driver said, like he had been waiting to be asked it. 'Keeps it from getting too cold in winter and too hot in summer.'

'For all the summer you're going to get in this place.'

'Oh, it's not here,' said the driver, a quarter turn of the head in Herbie's direction, 'it's Iran.'

Herbie must have shot him a glance. The driver smiled. 'My mother's side, only they still call it Persia. I was surprised myself first time I went there, thought I was going to stick out like a sore thumb, but no, not a bit. Everywhere I went there was a whole heap of people looked just like me. Up in the northeast, this is, near the border with Afghanistan.' He moved his left elbow a fraction, the cipher of a nudge. 'Out of the frying pan into the fire, what?' He said it again a couple of times more, under his breath – 'Out of the frying pan... Out of the frying pan' – before drifting into silence.

Herbie was content to let it settle. He moved his tongue behind his teeth, trying to conjure again the sensation of another's.

'Just past those traffic lights there,' he said at length. 'Then first on your right.'

The driver nodded, hit the indicator, and as though he had been on pause and had now pressed play again said, 'Here's the funny thing. See in Iran? I'm the big landowner. Here? Piece of dirt – worse than dirt – the way some of the punters treat you. Students are the worst, the girls and the fellas both. I'd make the whole lot of them do a class their first week there, How to Act Like a Reasonable Human Being Even When You've Had a Skinful.'

'This is me here,' said Herbie.

The driver stopped the meter. Five thirty. 'Call it a fiver dead.'

'You'll be a long time building your bungalow that way.'

The driver made a minute adjustment to the angle of his seat, took a drink from the bottle. 'Another day or two of this isn't going to kill me.'

Herbie wished he could be so certain. He let himself in, out of habit, rather than ringing the bell. He was conscious of a fumbling on the other side as he put his hand on the handle of the living-room door.

'I wasn't expecting to see you home so soon,' Beth said, sitting up straighter on the sofa. In fairness she looked like she meant it, facemask on, dressing gown on, foam dividers between her nail-varnished toes, bottles, jars, cotton wool wipes on the towel that took up the sofa's remaining cushions. 'Did you at least have fun while it lasted?'

'It was nice, yeah. No, it was.' Louise had kissed him. Draped her arms about his neck and kissed him. 'Really nice.'

He passed through into the kitchen to switch on the kettle, came out again a second later, sniffing the air.

'Have you been smoking dope?'

He thought he could see the colour rise even through the facemask's avocado. The Busted Blush. She dug her hand into her dressing-gown pocket and drew out from among the balled Kleenex a little brass pipe.

He took it from her. It looked like it had come off a radiator. It smelt (nose to the blackened bowl) like a room in his life he had forgotten was ever there.

'I don't suppose you've any left?'

'You serious?'

'Well, I've never used one of these before, but, yeah, why not?'

The mask cracked. 'Give us it here,' she said. 'And just so's you know, nobody says dope any more.'

It was too hot to be pleasant, was his first reaction, too hot certainly to be able to hold in enough to have any effect. He had a second try. 'I'm not sure this is going to work for me,' he said and then the clock moved on half an hour and Beth was refilling the bowl again and mentioning, a propos of something that in the next moment escaped him entirely, a London friend who was knocked down on the way home from the pub crossing a road... well, dual carriageway, which was stupid obviously, but the nearest footbridge was half a mile away and anyway he had done it loads of times before, just never when there was some oul lad trying to retune his car radio to Radio 4 – he had only just got DAB and kept brushing the channel change with his sleeve when he went to change gears – it was that sensitive – and thump!

Killed outright.

Twenty-five years of age, youngest child, only son, his parents, you can imagine, completely destroyed.

Herbie could imagine it all too well, or thought he could, but Beth was only getting started.

The mother in particular couldn't reconcile herself, kept coming back to the neighbourhood where her son had been living, wanting to talk to the people he was with that night, trying to break down those last hours into minutes, the minutes into seconds, the seconds into fractions, as if by delving deeper and deeper she would stop all forward motion and never actually arrive at the point where the oul lad looked up from his tinkering with the DAB and saw – too late – her beautiful twenty-five-year-old boy frozen in the headlights, the look of surprise that was still on his face, closed eyelids notwithstanding, as he lay in the mortuary... What way did he turn his head when he said that thing about childhood family holidays before leaving the bar? And did he smile? Was it that little sideways smile – his secret smile, his daddy always used to call it – the eyebrow on the opposite side going up involuntarily, which even if you couldn't see his mouth was a giveaway... all that sort of thing, over and over, and over.

It got so she was never away from there, going out with his friends to pubs and clubs – they were hardly going to tell her to get lost, were they? – and then the next thing she had left her husband and she had started seeing this guy that her son had been with right before he ran out into the road, though 'seeing' didn't really do it justice – pretty torrid, it was, and she had taken to doing things too like wearing her son's old camelhair coat, his shirts, his jumpers, this pair of vintage Lee jeans he had with *big* turn-ups. It wasn't that she wanted to *be* him exactly. She just wanted to be *one* with him.

'It all got too much in the end,' Beth said.

Herbie declined her offer of the pipe. 'Sounds to me like it was too much from the start.'

'I suppose until you've been there yourself…'

Please, please, never let me be. 'I suppose.'

'Anyway, the guy couldn't take it any more. Another week, he'd have been ready for the madhouse. And she – she very nearly got her wish for oneness with her son, took a razor to her wrists one night lying in the bath with his Lee jeans on and his favourite Hole T-shirt.'

'Hole?'

'Band. Courtney Love, was married to Kurt Cobain of…'

'Him I know.'

'Right. Well, she bolloxed it completely of course. All she managed to do was squirt blood all up the walls. Her husband came to pick her up, absolutely mortified, you know, one of those men, all his life he had known the right thing to do, and now…'

'Not.'

'And now not at all, no. Not a flipping baldy. About the only word he could get out was sorry. You'd have thought from the way he said it he was apologising for his whole life and hers.'

Much, much later, the pipe long since set aside, coals grown grey and cold, she said, 'That friend of mine who died?'

'Out on the road.'

'Mm. The guy who was with him that night? That wasn't a guy, that was me.'

'I had started to think that… So all the other stuff?'

'Well, if it wasn't a guy it can't have happened to him.'

And that was the last she ever talked about it.

6

Paul hadn't been back to Sam's since the night of his run-in with the brigadier, getting on for a month and a half ago now, and since the morning after, when Yolanda rang to see how he was keeping ('fine, I'm absolutely fine'), hadn't spoken to any of the regulars. Emmet had made a point of calling at the house a couple of times, when he was cleaning bins the next street over, but Paul was never in, or, if he was, he never answered.

'Saw the sister-in-law – or I take it it was her – peeking out the blinds,' he said after his second visit, and repeated what Yolanda said when she'd driven Paul home. 'A weird set-up, that.'

Herbie got the address from them and caught the bus up there one evening on his way from the Records Office. The house was of a type in which the east of the city particularly abounded, built, in stone, in the late-late 1910s for soldiers returning from the First World War. (Those that is who were able to walk back into their old way of life. For those who were not, then or afterwards, there was the Somme Hospital tucked away in the trees on the extreme eastern edge of town.) The plots were generous for the times: recompense for the cramped and filthy conditions the returning heroes had lived in the past four years, and in all likelihood, the vast majority of them, in the years before they enlisted too. Inevitably most of the extra space had in time been eaten into by driveways and garages, timber to begin with, then cement block and – most substantial but least sympathetic to the original building materials – unrendered red brick. Some of those garages had themselves been augmented, becoming fully incorporated extensions. And some had just had bits stuck on top, more or – as in the case of Paul's – less coherently.

There were a couple of fairly major cracks in the steps leading up to his front door. The jagged line where they met the side of the garage was etched in bright green slime.

From the little outer landing before the front door Herbie had an uninterrupted view still further east to the parliament buildings, clinging to the side of the Craigantlet Hills, rising above the tree line of Stormont estate. The image came back to him of the stripped-out Portakabin abandoned on the Upper Springfield Road.

Ungivers of Fuck.

He rapped the door. Waited. Rapped again. Not a sound. He walked back down the steps and round the front of the garage to the house door. His finger on the bell unleashed a piece of Mozart but was otherwise unproductive. He had noticed, as he approached, a wrought-iron gate on the other side of the house, filling the narrow space between it and the redbrick wall of the extension next door.

He wasn't sure what possessed him to open it now. Walk up the passageway. Round the back of the house. Somebody else's house. *Their* house, the man and the woman – he saw them through the window – in full-length aprons, leaning in over a table spread with newspapers on which lay… Actually, Herbie had no idea what. Apart from the fact it was the width of his own thigh but twice as long, tapering to a point at either end. And black, with orange flashes, which they were still touching in with paintbrushes.

The man looked up. Paul's face, add ten and take away something vital.

'I'm sorry,' Herbie said towards the small window open on the latch. 'I was looking for Paul.'

It was the woman who spoke. 'Paul has his own flat.'

'He wasn't answering his door.'

'He must be out. He has his own life too.'

The man – the brother – had already returned to dabbing at the model, as Herbie now supposed it to be, with his brush. From what depths Herbie did not know, the term 'Cigar Ship' floated to the surface of his mind.

'Would you go now, please?' the woman said. 'This is private property.'

'I just wanted to know how he was doing. If you see him would you tell him…' He didn't finish. Of course they wouldn't tell him anything. He turned towards the passage. Turned back. 'Did you not hear *your* bell?'

'We weren't expecting anyone.'

He walked back round the front of the house and up the steps beside the garage a second time. The only thing he could find to write on was his bus ticket. Paul, he wrote, give me a call, Herbie, and added his number before slipping the ticket under the door.

He was never in his life so glad to leave anywhere.

It was Beth who caught up with Paul in the end, a week or so later. 'I just brought a book with me and sat on my bag at the top of the stairs until he came back,' she told Herbie that evening as they were unwrapping dinner (one cod supper, one scampi and small chips). 'He asked me in for coffee. It's actually a really nice wee flat he has there. Well, bedsit. A bit draughty round the ankles. I don't know that they've insulated the garage ceiling very well. At all, maybe. I think he's a bit embarrassed, how it all looks, him living up there with not even his own meter box. Yolanda must have really gone to town on the brother and his wife over that. He told me they lost their parents when he was still at school. His brother was already married. It seemed like a good solution at the time. Anyway, he said he was dead sorry he hadn't been in touch with anyone. Just, you know, one thing and another.'

'Vinegar?' Herbie asked.

'I'm all right.'

Paul had given up the Uber. That was the big news. Or the Uber had given him up: no car, no shifts, no buts, no ifs. All he walked away with from that whole business was the scrap value of his car. At least it gave him a couple of weeks to look around.

'So, what's he doing now?'

'Pizza delivery.'

'Ah, come on.'

'What do you mean, come on?'

'I mean it's good he's got something, but, I don't know, like it wasn't so long ago he was talking about some management fast-track programme he was on… He looked set.'

Beth raised an eyebrow at that. 'Seriously, Dad? *Set*? Did you not know, they've taken that one out of the dictionary?'

He cut into his cod. He thought how rarely this moment disappointed. Every fish looked like the ideal of fish rather than the fish itself. And how quickly, once he started to eat, the experience palled.

Beth popped half a scampi into her mouth. 'Fo' wha' i's wo- wo—,' she said, then stopped to draw in air, cool the fish, chew, 'for – what – it's – *worth*, he did tell me delivering pizzas was not exactly what he had fantasised about doing when he was a wee lad, but then neither was living over the garage of his brother's house. But you know, needs must, and the pizza place provides the van. Here he was to me, let whoever wants to run into me now: not my problem.' She moved a chip about the plate, gathering salt. 'You can see the attraction. I told him if I had my licence I'd maybe be joining him.'

'What do you mean *if* you had your licence?'

He was as certain as he could be of anything he hadn't misremembered that. The week leading up to her test, Tanya taking her out for extra lessons, on the basis that she was the less likely to panic in the passenger seat, coming home one of the nights ashen-faced. 'She hasn't a hope in hell.'

So of course she walked it. Drove it. Practically flawlessly.

'Oh,' she said now. 'Did I not say? Ah. I lost it.'

'How?'

'How do you think?'

'Not drink?'

'Not drink, no. The other.' She mimed a pipe. 'Thirteen miles an hour in a fifty zone. Four in the morning, like, not a sinner about. Not another one. Unless you count the cops. I'm not proud. It's not been a great year, but you know if I can pack all this crap into twelve months, get it out of the way...' She held the heavily salted chip poised before her mouth. 'I'll maybe think about giving these up too.' She chewed a moment then smiled. 'Nah.'

It was still early when Herbie turned out of his street on to the main road the next day. A September morning to stand for all September mornings. Cloudless, sky-high sky-blue sky, all earthly things put in their place, the limits – of hills and buildings alike – darkly delineated.

He glimpsed over the roof of a delivery van a long-necked metal crook nuzzling the leaves and petals of a basket hanging from the lamppost level with the Post Office. Looking down he saw that the footpath was wet around the base of the lampposts nearer to him – the undersides of the baskets, when he glanced up again, dripping – and sure enough, as the delivery van indicated and pulled away, there was the man from the council gripping the metal crook, left-handed, while his right hand played out the hose that joined it to a plastic tank mounted on the bed of a truck with the council's crest on the door. There were dead heads on the tarmac at his feet. From the splay of them it might have been the fall that killed them. Herbie didn't see this man more than two or three times in the year, and always unexpectedly, which only added to the delight he took at the sight of him. He looked this morning, as he always looked, as though he had stepped through a tear in the space–time continuum: yes, he had the flatbed truck (new-looking too since the last time Herbie saw him) and the big green plastic tank on the back, but the rest of him, the wellie boots, tan bib-and-brace dungarees, one strap perpetually undone, the woolly hat pushed back off his forehead, seemed to belong to another era, of lamp-lighters and knocker-uppers (the dungarees were one shade off sepia). He walked his pole to the next lamppost, just down from the bakery, turning it so that the nozzle didn't drip until it was safely in among the plants again, where he watched it like a thing joined to him by something stronger than steel. Look at you, how good you are at doing that, his expression said as the crook worked its way around. People passed – Herbie passed eventually – but the man only had eyes, only ever had eyes, for what was going on over all their heads.

In a few minutes he would be packed up and gone to another part of the city and that would be the last Herbie or anyone else round here would see of him till winter or beyond. More power to you. Keep on the move. One step ahead of the hirers and firers and rationalisers. Don't stop until you choose to.

Past the Catch-phrase church Herbie went, whistling ('Hit me with your rhythm stick', arrived at unconsciously via 'Reasons to Be Cheerful, Part 3': 'hanging basket tenders, overall suspenders... chrys-an-the-mums'), downhill into what a couple of hundred years before had been estuary mud and only ten years before tight-packed Victorian kitchen houses finally beginning to fall in on themselves. There was landscaping going on along the banks of the river that ran transversely beneath the road, all the trolleygators and wide-mouthed bagfish culled. A couple of inner-city ducks surfaced, shaking their heads, and turned tight circles as though still trying to figure out where their erstwhile river mates had gone.

He wondered whether Beth might not be on to something, getting all the crap out of the way in one go. Though twelve months...? Things had accelerated in a generation. 'Give it five years,' was what he and Tanya had used to say, 'and if it doesn't work out, well, no odds.' Five years then as lightly tossed away as a beaten hand of cards.

'How's it going?'

He had advanced to just short of the Dee Street Bridge. A man stood before him. His own age, give or take. Beard. Big smile. It took Herbie a moment – or a sentence – to place him. 'I was looking out for you at the game on Saturday,' the man said. Of course, the couple of steps down in the football ground.

'I wasn't able,' said Herbie. (Why?) 'Work. How'd they get on?'

'You didn't hear? Won.' He held up a finger: *wait for it.* 'Seven goals to two.'

'Seven to two?' It sounded more like the odds you would have got against them scoring even once, the time Herbie saw them, if they had played on till Sunday. 'Maybe I should stay away every week.'

'Sure who cares about the football? If we were bothered about that we'd all have given up going years ago. It's being there, isn't it? Even when you're getting chinned. Let the glory-hunters trot over to England every weekend. Well for them they have the money, what? Though they'll never see in a lifetime what yon Premier League players earn in a year.'

'You're right there.'

'Sure I know I am.'

He clapped Herbie on the upper arm. 'See you at the next one,' he said and dandered on.

Herbie was nearing the crest of the bridge when he heard it. 'Herbie, Herbie, give us a wave!' Your man was down below, in one of the cul-de-sacs running off to the left, hands cupped either side of his mouth and nose. 'Herbie... give us a wave!'

Herbie waved, a big, broad, over-the-head sweep. Your man gave him the thumbs up and they each carried on their way.

Two mornings later he opened the front door to torrential

rain. He made it as far as the main road before deciding no harm would come from letting the Past get another day older before he disturbed it again and was about to turn again for home when he noticed that the sign outside the Post Office had changed from 'To Let' to 'Acquired for Client'.

'Not the first idea,' Derek said when he went into Sam's to ask who this client might be.

No more, it seemed, had any of the Post Office staff. 'Start of February, that's all Neeta says they have been told.'

'But it's definitely another restaurant?' Herbie asked.

'To quote Neeta? "I haven't heard that it isn't."'

Neeta had heard though, from a couple of the other counter staff, that there were already people making enquiries – 'queuing up specially to enquire, I mean' – about how they could book for the opening night. 'They probably think it would be worth the gamble: even if the place turns out to be shit at least they can tell everyone they were the first to find out.'

Talking of gambles, the bookie's at the far end of the road was already taking bets on which TV chef's name was going over the door. ('Oh, God,' said Neeta, 'don't tell me I started that.') Ruby Tandoh was streets ahead.

Which taken all together made it the worst possible moment (not that there was ever a particularly good one) for the rat thing to happen.

Derek, as he had cause to recount it many times later, came out through the archway dark and early one mid-October morning, cigarette at the ready, to find a two-foot-long specimen lying, stiff and first-frost-spangled, in the middle of the yard. His initial thought was that it had come over the yard wall already dead – a message – and if Sam, whose first and favourite task of every day was to turn the sign on the door from 'Closed' to 'Open', hadn't called him from the kitchen at that moment he would have had his phone out taking pictures, or phoning the PSNI – the BBC. Hate crime!

'Quick,' Sam shouted, 'come and see.'

He was standing in front of the dishwasher. 'There.' A small cluster of raisin-shaped droppings. 'Here, take you that end.' Together they manoeuvred the dishwasher far enough out from under the countertop that they could see in behind. 'Ah, no.'

The wires were chewed, the outlet pipe too. There was a hole in the skirting beside it the size of your fist. More droppings.

'You had better go and turn the sign on the door again,' Derek said.

So of course customers started sending texts and posting on their Facebook page – 'Hope all OK'. When they didn't open on the second day (to 'Closed' had now been added 'Due to Circumstances Beyond Our Control') the rumours began to fly, shrinking on the third day to a single rumour, irrefutably rat-shaped.

The Belfast Rolling Roadworks Revue – now in its fourteenth year – had rumbled round to their bottleneck of the woods a few weeks before. More than likely that was what had caused the infestation, the young woman who came out to do the initial inspection told them. Sam queried the word 'infestation'.

Rats, the inspector said, were not famed for their

solitariness. She had pushed her hygiene mask up on to the top of her head, a novelty party hat. 'All it takes is one fractured sewer pipe. Complete lottery after that where they will pop up.'

'Just our luck that that would be the one lottery we'd actually win,' said Derek.

'Of all the sewers in all the pipes in all this city it had to come climbing out of ours.'

'Something like that,' the inspector said. 'Have you a bin where I can put these gloves?'

She returned a moment later, pointing over her shoulder with her thumb. 'You know someone has spelt…'

'DICK with the Scrabble tiles?' Sam said and jerked his own thumb. 'Talk to the man who bought them.'

It took the environmental people until the middle of the following month just to get to the source of the problem. The whole kitchen floor had to be dug up, half the yard too. There was collateral damage to walls and doorframes. The kitchen plumbing was all going to have to be redone. Sam and Derek abandoned the place to the builders and spent their days instead shuttling between the Department of the Environment and their own solicitor, who gave them the bad news finally that the most they could hope for out of this was to recoup the cost of the actual repairs. The lost trade, and the cash that would have flowed from it? Just that, lost.

'The best thing you could do,' he said, 'is take a wee cottage somewhere well away from all this and plot your grand reopening.'

7

Herbie and Louise left it in the end till the fourth date, which between the jigs and the reels came a full two months after the first, before they slept together. Her apartment, in a converted villa next door to an Over-55s compound, whose big selling point apparently was the walking path round the perimeter. ('I've watched them,' Louise said to Herbie. 'And do you know the scariest thing? *They all walk in the same direction.*') It was, in the circumstances, and given all the possibilities for awkwardness or embarrassment, an immense, and intense, relief as much as pleasure.

'Next time,' she said, 'we can try it with our clothes off, and maybe' – rearranging the duvet they had trailed off in their near miss – 'actually on the bed.' Which was what they did at his, later that week, an afternoon when he knew Beth would not be home, and several subsequent afternoons and evenings as the nights drew in, not forgetting the foggy morning she picked him up from the corner of his street in her car and drove him to a lane off a road off a bigger road off the M2 and, true to the words she had uttered when she switched off the engine and turned to face him, fucked his brains out. That promise aside, they almost never spoke while they were making love – an eavesdropper would have had to infer from the gap between words what they were about – but that too was a relief. The store of words they had each built up over the years, for parts and their uses, could only ever be a foreign language to the other. (That 'fuck your brains out' had come with quotation marks and in a borrowed drawl.) They communicated better by look and gesture, and touch. They didn't talk much either, afterwards or before, about what this all amounted to. Let things proceed as they will, at their own pace, was the unspoken agreement.

'I think you're doing the right thing,' Beth told him when, cornered by her questioning about how he and Louise were getting on, he had come out with that last sentence.

'You don't want to be putting yourselves under a whole lot of pressure,' said Tanya, to whom Beth had spoken, within a couple of hours, must have been, of her speaking to him. ('She asked me outright if you were seeing anybody. What am I supposed to do, lie?') 'I mean,' Tanya said, 'I was lucky, I knew the minute I laid eyes on Martin he was the one. I told him that first night we had sex, don't even think about doing this unless you mean it to be for ever…'

He wondered if she remembered the five-year plans, or if he had got it all wrong and it was only he who had made them.

'Though where we had got to at that moment,' Tanya went on, 'if he'd said he *didn't*, I think I'd have had to take matters into my own hands, if you get my…'

'I get,' he said more shrilly than he meant, and when she told him she was only trying to help, added a 'thank you' and 'I will store all this away,' before steering the conversation on to Beth. 'Was she telling you about the job?'

'Sounds like she's landed on her feet... finally.'

Beth's search for work had taken her via a day in a vape store ('Seriously? If I wanted to spend that much time surrounded by sad men I'd have been an MP'), a week in a newly opened hi-tech dry-cleaner's (the tech crashed, the cleaner's closed) to a film location services company – New Eyes NI – whose founders, a brother and sister from out in the wilds of Tyrone (their term), had grown up making no-budget horror flicks on the family farm, turning slurry pits and gauze-covered torches into moonlit lagoons, Barbies into Barbie zombies, and had come to Belfast thinking if people the world over were wetting themselves over the Dark Hedges there was easy money to be made.

'Wait till they see what Tyrone has to offer,' the sister told Beth, 'they'll come in their pants.'

(Herbie held up a hand. 'You're familiar with the phrase "too much detail"?'

'I'm trying to give you an impression of her,' said Beth.)

Beth explained to them at the interview – as she had at every interview she had attended – about her bankruptcy.

'We'll keep you away from the books then,' the sister said. Her name was Roza, short for Rozabela. Micky, her brother, was Mihhaelo on his birth certificate. Their parents were practising Esperantists, Tyrone's two (become four) and only.

'At least you gave it a go,' Micky said. 'You know what it's like running a business.'

She explained to them too about the driving ban.

'Micky and I do the actual locations,' Roza said. 'All we want is someone to sit in the office and answer this bloody phone and how they get here is their own business, they could pogo for all we care.'

The office was on a former industrial estate – now enterprise zone – in an old lemonade bottling plant that had become, for a turn-of-the-Millennium time, the headquarters of a video rental chain before morphing again into a hub for film-related businesses, of which there were nearly as many varieties as there had once been flavours of lemonade. There were production companies, facilities companies, extras companies, human and equine, animation companies, editing companies, and a company that hired out offices to companies that needed a Northern Ireland address for the funding applications to enable them to acquire an office permanently, or at least until the end of post-production.

And as Roza had intimated, the phone in the New Eyes NI office (Beth most days walked to be at its beck and call) needed answering a lot. Even if you discounted the people who were just looking for directions – 'That's not the kind of locations service we provide... have you tried Google Maps?' – there were a serious number of overseas producers interested in bringing in their films to (you could hear them sometimes pausing to make sure they were getting it right)

Northern Ireland. Micky and Roza were interested in enticing as many of them as possible out of Belfast and into Tyrone. *In their pants, I'm telling you. In their actual pants.*

The highest of their hopes to date was for a German-Polish (soon to be – if the locations could be found – German-Polish-Northern-Irish) co-production set against the backdrop of the border disputes, and consequent uprisings, in Upper Silesia in the years after the First World War.

The script called for a restaging, midway through the second act, of the battle of Annaberg, in which a combination of German Freikorps and ethnically German Poles succeeded in dislodging Polish insurgents from a hilltop monastery commanding the approach to the whole Oder valley.

'There's as much action in the boudoir, like, as there is on the battlefield,' Roza said.

'They actually use the word boudoir in the script,' Micky chipped in, 'about once every two pages.'

'If we can't find them a hill in the Sperrins to run up and down shooting their guns, I'm sure we can find them a four-poster bed and some fancy drapes if they want to keep the rating down. And we do have a genuine border we can offer them.'

'Genuine disputed border.'

'If they need to, you know, get in the zone.'

'They're nuts the pair of them,' Beth told Herbie. 'The whole business is nuts. But, sure, if nothing else it will keep me out of trouble for a while.'

Which was almost word for word what Tanya said before

she rang off. A modest enough ambition, but, he supposed, if you had been as low as his daughter had been, you had to start again building from somewhere.

There was always a bit of a lull at the Records Office in the autumn when the cruise ships left and the tourist numbers dropped, though with every passing year – every new colour supplement feature and *Lonely Planet* accolade – the drop was a little less steep. The freelance researchers counted the days. Sure, the tourists ensured there was plenty of work to go around – to say nothing of the tips – but most of them if pressed would have told you they preferred having the place more or less to themselves and the time to pursue their own projects as the year wound slowly down.

So, of course, someone in the upper reaches had gone and had the bright idea this year of putting on a series of lunchtime lectures – 'research showcases' – to pull more people in.

Herbie and the other researchers gathered in the cafe to watch as Briony from HR – 'Brisk Briony', behind her back – wrote the dates of six consecutive Tuesdays on strips of paper, rolled them tight and tossed them into an empty Lavazza tin.

'How do we decide who draws first?' someone asked.

'I point at you,' Briony said. Briskly.

She pointed at Herbie third. He pulled out the date of the penultimate Tuesday, which happened also to be the penultimate Tuesday of November.

'What do you want to call that?' Briony asked. '"An Illustrated Guide to Tithe Applotments"?'

Pete cupped a hand to his ear. 'Listen,' he said, 'you can already hear the stampeding feet… going the other way.'

Briony pointed at him. 'Now you.' He drew week three.

'Ooh,' said Lydia. 'The Difficult Third Lecture.'

Pete rolled the paper into a ball and flicked it at her with his thumb. 'Wee buns,' he said.

The Deputy Lord Mayor arrived with her entourage on Coca-Cola-Zero-branded Belfast Bikes to launch the series and referred disconcertingly in her words of welcome to her great-grandfather's experiences as a child evacuee following the Blitz of April 1941. Herbie missed the next couple of sentences as he tried to do the maths. Child meaning sixteen or under in '41, born 1925 at the earliest, another two generations between him and her, making her… twenty-five? Tops? When he tuned in again, she was expanding on what she called the Next Iteration of the city's development.

'The council's target is to double the value of tourism spend by 2030.'

('That's ambitious,' Lydia whispered, and flashed up the time on her phone, 'it's already 13.07.') The cruise ships were all well and good, but too many visitors apparently were still coming in for a night and two days, a lightning raid up on the coach or train from Dublin, round the same handful of attractions before escaping South again. 'We in the City Hall are working closely with the tourism sector to deliver world-class three- to five-day Belfast city breaks, but in the short term our goal is to persuade every visitor to stay just one more night.' Someone behind Herbie crooned the last three words, Phil Collins style. 'You, here, obviously have an important role to play in this,' the Deputy Lord Mayor said. 'We see particular room for growth among the culturally curious across both these islands and of course Belfast does have a Unique Product that we should not shy away from promoting, as long as it is done in a sympathetic way.'

She didn't need to spell out what that unique product was. Twenty-five years in making (or eight hundred, depending on who you asked), twenty-five years and counting in the fixing. As to what constituted a sympathetic way of promoting it... Herbie was ruling out diesel cubes.

There must have been a hundred and twenty in the room to hear her, including press and her own entourage, a few of whom looked the worse for the mile-long cycle from City Hall, with still a mile-long cycle ahead of them to get back.

The subject of the lecture itself was rather neatly (too neatly, Briony?) tourism, to this very spot in fact, going back to the mid-nineteenth century.

Pauline, who had picked week one out of the Lavazza tin, signed the lecture while Kofi, her... (left forefinger straight up, right forefinger coming in from wide to join it) *sidekick*, he decided, translated. Between them they described how when the land had first been reclaimed it had been given over entirely to pleasure – a People's Park, complete with Ferris wheel and scaled-down version of the Crystal Palace (and brambles, Herbie wanted to say, don't forget the brambles), before shipbuilding got a toe-hold and in fairly short order pushed everything else out.

How apt, she and Kofi said, a heartbeat apart, that the latest and perhaps greatest attraction of this new era of tourism – *Titanic* Belfast – should in its glass-walled way nod to its 1850s predecessor. In cities as in life, we might conclude (Pauline did, so Kofi did too), what goes around comes around, and what goes down can triumphantly rise again. It was as rousing a phrase to see as to hear and completely for the moment made Herbie forget that he had previously heard Pauline refer to the *Titanic* building as an eyesore.

If her going first had been a fix, he had to admit, it had been an inspired one.

The week after – no press now, no Deputy Mayoral entourage – there were still close to eighty in attendance for a talk on amateur boxing and the archive. (You could, in fairness, never go wrong in Belfast with boxing.) The week after that – Pete's week, the Difficult Third – the audience was still in single figures ten minutes before the lecture ('Speaking to the Nation? Broadcasting in a Fractured State') was due to begin, though it climbed eventually to nineteen, one of whom got up when it came to the Q&A and delivered a ten-minute lecture of his own while a friend distributed leaflets. The fourth Tuesday was Lydia, the Women's Solemn League and Covenant, which was always bound to be good, if perhaps a little one-sided, box office. 'We, whose names are underwritten, women of Ulster, and loyal subjects of our gracious King, being firmly persuaded that Home Rule would be disastrous to our Country, desire to associate ourselves with the men of Ulster in their uncompromising opposition to the Home Rule Bill now before Parliament, whereby it is proposed to drive Ulster out of her cherished place in the Constitution of the United Kingdom, and to place her under the domination and control of a Parliament in Ireland. Praying that from this calamity God will save Ireland, we here to subscribe our names.'

Seventy-seven, they got for that, and late Twitter apologies from a group of women from Londonderry – they were very particular about the first two syllables – whose minibus had got a flat tyre at a roundabout outside Magherafelt, from where they tweeted a photo of themselves with a banner reading 'Leave Means Leave'. (And perhaps Leave enough time for unforeseen sharp objects on the road if you ever mean to Arrive.)

Then it was week five and Herbie.

He had thought, several times in the previous month, about changing tack and taking as the subject of his talk Sean's notebooks, but he and Louise were just starting then to see more of each other. Between that and Beth coming home in the evenings, full of tales of Screen, his time was no longer entirely his own. Who knew, once he opened those boxes and started to read, what he would unearth and how long it would take him to sift and organise it? Besides, the fliers had already gone out with that 'Illustrated Guide to' title on them and he had a hunch that Pete was not wrong about the numbers it would attract. Would he really have been doing justice to

Sean's memory by unveiling the work of nearly forty years to half a dozen people?

The weather, that Tuesday, was Belfast Bland – available any given season of the year, more an absence of extremes than the presence of anything you could put a name to – which ought to have been a good thing: who wanted to have to brave the wind and the rain for the pleasure of giving up their lunch hour? (It had practically been blowing a gale – Met Office amber warning – in week three, as Pete had reminded Herbie several times since.) On the other hand, people might step out from their houses or workplaces into the milder-than-recent air and think, wait a minute, this is too pleasant a day this time of year to spend cooped up in a lecture room. And there was of course always the possibility that no matter what the weather, no matter the number and quality of illustrations, they just could not give a flying fuck for tithe applotments.

He went down to the lecture room, just to the right of the lobby, three quarters of an hour before he was due to start, to check it was all in order. The caterers arrived, while he was there, with sandwiches, three platefuls of them, bent out of shape by the cling film, the tea and coffee flasks, setting one of each on the table, either side of the sandwiches, and tucking their twins away underneath as back-up. You couldn't fault them for optimism.

They had just left the room when he heard a series of shrill cries from outside. He crossed to the window and saw through the fence across the road, behind which lay a patch of purest brownfield, the seagull chick rising above a melee of crows with a fat chip already halfway down its gullet. It had grown now to two-thirds the size of the parents, all hint of cuteness buried beneath a mess of brown and grey feathers. The crows flapped and cawed, but the chick flapped harder and gulped faster: one – two – three – gone. It lifted off and landed again a few yards away to preen, chip grease mingling with its own body's oils. A picture of self-satisfaction.

He went and stood at the lectern to run through the PowerPoint, matching images to text recited silently in his head. Sandy from tech support came in just as he was finishing. She had had a tattoo done since last he had seen her, a small pink rose about to blossom, high up on her right cheek bone. The stem, running from the hinge of her jaw, was formed from the words *just live* in thorny cursive.

'You look like you've got it all in hand,' she said. 'Just one other thing… See this?' A multicoloured rope of cables as thick as his forearm leading up from the floor into the lectern's hardware. 'Don't, whatever you do, touch that with your foot.'

'Are you afraid I'm going to wipe out the entire country's memory?'

Sandy smiled the smile of the terminally unamused. The rose twitched. 'Just be sure and don't touch it.'

He got eighteen – he counted them as they came through the door, him and Pete both, clearly. He dug Herbie in the ribs before taking his seat. 'Looks like I'm not going to finish bottom of the league after all, even though the weather was on your side.'

'I didn't know it was a competition.'

'Oh, I'm sure you did,' said Pete. 'Where's the fun in it otherwise?'

'There's still next week, don't forget.'

'"A Canter Through Couture"? With a college of further education sitting on our doorstep offering fashion courses? I wouldn't be pinning my hopes on that one coming up short.'

Herbie was still on his introductory remarks – was that old boy in the third row already asleep? – when the door opened and a nineteenth person, Beth, slipped in and took the first seat that presented itself, at the back of the room, although all eighteen other heads turned anyway – well, seventeen did (he was asleep, no question).

She clapped at the end loudly enough for another ten.

As they stood afterwards eating sandwiches and drinking coffee (second flask not required, nor all of the first one) Herbie introduced her to those of his colleagues who had made it along.

'So *you're* Joint-Last Pete,' she said and shook his hand. Evidently she had been counting too.

'Like father like daughter, I see,' said Pete, taking his hand back and clapping Herbie, a fraction too hard, between the shoulder blades.

'So, explain to me again why you like working here so much,' Beth said when he had gone.

That night Herbie dreamed he was back in the lecture room, back behind the lectern, naked of course from the waist down, apart from his shoes (his old school shoes), though he kept hoping that the audience, which – of course, of course – was twice the size at least of the first week, twice as many councillors and cameras, wouldn't notice... if he could just turn the lectern a little more to the left, no, wait, to the right... any damn direction at all. He pressed down with the heels of his hands, gripping the corners nearest to him, but the lectern wouldn't budge, and the audience meanwhile seemed somehow to have moved closer, to have begun to filter in around the sides, any second now one of them was bound to say something, especially as he was – oh, God, he really was – stiffening. He gripped the lectern tighter – felt the strain right up in his shoulders – and wrenched it... wrenched again. There was a sound – *phht* – like a gas jet cutting out, which even as he dreamed it struck him as a curious anachronism, for he knew exactly the technological consequences of what he had done. He looked down between his feet at the rope of coloured cables... Sliced clean through, writhing, two snakes where before there was one. He didn't care now who knew he had nothing on underneath – was sticking right out in front of him – he dropped to his hands and knees, toppling the lectern as he did... he had to get the two ends of this thing back together before any permanent damage was done. Already though he was aware of chairs being knocked over as the audience stampeded for the door out to the corridor, from where he could hear more panicked footsteps, shouts... The lights flickered, once, twice, three times, then failed. The fire alarms went off all through the building, followed a rapid heartbeat later by the car alarms out in the car park, scores of them, hundreds maybe, right the way down to the SSE Arena, sirens cutting in and out of them, converging from all four corners of the city. *Fuck, fuck, fuck.* He had the laces out of his shoes and was knotting them together or not knotting them – the aglets had come off and the fraying cords kept slipping from his grasp, no matter how much he licked his fingertips – and then he felt it, a tremor beneath him, faint at first but growing in magnitude. Such chairs as remained standing fell. Carpet tiles were dislodged, a crack appeared in the exposed floor to the right of where the lectern had landed. He watched, helpless, as it zigzagged the length of the floor and up the end wall, watched as the room and all the rooms above it split in two. His impression was that the entire city had started to crumble, its foundations eaten away, so that he was kneeling looking up into the heavens – it was definitely heavens, not sky – where he saw, of all the things in this world or the next that he might have seen, the face in one particular cloud of the man who owned the chemist's his parents had always favoured when he was growing up, frowning, the way he did when anyone handed him a prescription, as though whatever was ailing them had to be their own fault: *what have you gone and done now…?* And that was the end of it.

In the next version of the dream he had, only a few nights later, he went into the lecture theatre on purpose with a long-handled axe up the sleeve of his coat and whacked the cables – and whacked them and whacked them – until the security guards, friends of his all, came running into the room, whereupon he turned the axe – it was a light sabre now – on them.

The thought occurred to him again, reconstructing the dream in the cold, cold still-not-light of 7 a.m. (he hadn't yet got round to resetting the timer on the radiators after the clocks went back): it might be time he found something else to do with his days.

Roza and Micky had found the ideal hill for the German-Polish producers to have their Annaberg battle on, rising up from a wind-blasted bog just north of Killeter, a couple of miles from the border with County Donegal. 'There's an old bit of a ruin on it that can easily be built up to look like a monastery,' Roza said. 'They can shoot it in reverse: start with the aftermath, then have all the fighting and the killing, then finish up by making it all better again.'

'Then go on from there and do the rest of the twentieth century,' said Micky. 'The rest of recorded history, why not, right back to the Garden of Eden.'

'In Tyrone naturally,' Roza said.

The producers weren't hanging about. The call had gone out in the papers and across all the social media platforms for extras. Hundreds had come forward to enlist. 'There's only one problem,' Micky told Beth, who told Herbie, at the end of the first day, 'they all want to be insurgents.'

'Me play a member of the Freikorps?' one man said when he turned up at the location and was shown his uniform. 'You've got to be kidding. What if somebody recognised me dressed up as a Nazi?'

Roza pointed out that there was little likelihood of the film ever getting a UK and Ireland release and besides these were the very early days of National Socialism in Germany, it was unlikely that many of the Freikorps battalions were yet affiliated.

'Yeah, but people could still find it on YouTube.' Leaning closer then, 'And, like, even if they weren't Nazis they were still Huns.'

Huns, she took that to be, both in its German-soldier sense and in its more local, 'for thine is the kingdom, *the power and the glory*' usage.

Another group of would-be extras arrived in two identical vans and after half an hour's negotiation about which side they would be on, disembarked and formed up in three very well-drilled columns. After a further half hour scouting the terrain, their spokesperson took the director aside and advised her on how the insurgents could hold the hill, on condition that she let him take command.

'I'm afraid you have this the wrong way round: you have to lose,' the director said. The spokesperson suggested she have a chat with the writer. 'It's not about his script,' the director told him, 'it's about what actually happened: the Freikorps chase you and the rest of the insurgents down the other side of the hill.' At which point the spokesperson clicked his heels, said thanks but no thanks, and he and his well-drilled friends got back in their vans and drove away.

In the end the only way they could make the numbers work was to cast local people as Poles while recruiting the Freikorps almost entirely from actual Poles living in the larger towns roundabout. Beth visited the set one of the days they were shooting there, although by the time she had got across the bog in one direction and factored in the time needed to get back across it heading home, it was more like 'one of the hours'. She got chatting to two brothers from Chelm who had been living this past few years in Dungannon, working on a mushroom farm, and who told her this could well be the last thing they did before they were obliged to move to the Donegal side of the border in order to work, or else headed back home for good. They liked the fucked-up irony that they were going to be the ones doing the driving out.

'Though you know,' the older brother said and adjusted the peak of his Freikorps cap, 'that we Poles regrouped after Annaberg. We got them in the end.'

The battle raged, was reset, raged, was reset, and raged again for four full days. (The sound effects were added later, but the guide track – played over speakers hidden in boxes round the set – was actually a manipulated version of Halloween fireworks displays, which those who remembered said bore a striking resemblance to the Belfast gun battles of the early Seventies.) For three nights everyone bar the director and her DP got gloriously pissed on the campsite that the production company had erected on a neighbouring hill in order to save on accommodation and transport costs: Freikorps and insurgent, walking wounded and bloodily deceased, long established and recently arrived, swapping stories and songs, showing photos pulled up from smartphone wallets. And all the time the winds blew in raw off the Atlantic and almost unobstructed across Donegal. (It was supposed to be May. Luckily there wasn't a tree within a half-mile radius to give the lie to that.) When the director finally called a wrap her assistant passed among them with medals made out of flattened beer-bottle caps and the foil from the necks of cider bottles.

Then both sides united in electing a representative in case the political institutions at Stormont were ever revived. After all that savagery and bloodletting they reckoned they must surely have merited speaking rights in the chamber. At the very least a mural or two.

Or leave it another thirty years and there was bound to be a novel.

8

Herbie hadn't really bothered much with Christmas for the past few years. A tree, of course, there had to be a tree, which he would usually get around to putting up the day before Christmas Eve, but cards and all the rest of it…? Nah. Not for him.

Beth, though, was insistent. First of December equalled the first mince pie (as the second equalled the second, the third the third) and a wreath on the front door. He told her that he had seen interesting-looking wreaths when he was passing the Christmas Market (or Post-Halloween: it had been up for a fortnight already), birch twig possibly, with sloe berries, but Beth wouldn't hear of getting anything from there. A giant outdoor pub ringed by sub-M&S tat. ('Nothing wrong with M&S,' Herbie said.) And no birch twigs either: holly from the fruit and veg shop, or forget about it.

He stood inside chatting to the fruit and veg man while she looked at every wreath hanging from the awning – three times – before making up her mind, changing it, then changing back again: that one, definitely. And it was admittedly beautiful, a distillation almost of the form. With a bunch of mistletoe and a metre of red ribbon thrown in, gratis. 'You're my first of the year,' the fruit and veg man said.

She asked Herbie as they were tying the wreath to the door knocker whether he still did Black Santa. Not for a long while, was the honest answer.

The Dean of St Anne's Cathedral had started – way before Beth was born – keeping a vigil in the week leading up to Christmas, out on the footpath of Donegall Street at the bottom of the cathedral steps, a box beside him for donations to charity, and dressed in his dean's dark cape, the hood as often as not up against the weather (it was a wind tunnel, Donegall Street), hence the nickname.

It had become one of their Christmas Eve traditions, his and Beth's, pick up the turkey crown and then swing by Donegall Street, while Tanya caught up with old school friends, home for the holidays, in the bar in the Queen's Arcade. Beth – that's right – with the little satin drawstring bag containing the pocket money she had been putting aside since Halloween... in the zebra money box, he supposed. The solemnity with which she undid the string and shook out the coins, or as she got older the folded five-pound notes.

'Let's try and do it again this year,' Beth said.

'I don't mean to dilute the Christmas spirit...'

'But does he take IOUs?'

'I wouldn't have put it like that exactly. Do you need to check in with your receiver?'

'I keep telling you, Polly's cool with everything.'

He shut the front door. She took a couple of steps into the hallway, stopped. 'Wait, did I dream it, or did you tell me when I was small one of your uncles used to give you IOUs for Christmas?'

'He only did the once. Robin. He was always a wee bit odd, lived on his own.'

'Ah' – she turned her head this way and that and this again – 'have you looked around you lately?'

'Not odd *because* he lived on his own. Odd *and* he did. Most years he gave all us nephews a bottle of Brut. I must have been eight when I got my first one. Don't ask me what I got from him before that. Soap on a rope. Then one year, I don't know, maybe the Brut boat sank or was hijacked, he sent us an envelope, no card or anything, with an IOU...'

'... one bottle of Brut.'

'*Item*, one bottle of Brut, was how he wrote it. Brought the bottle round eventually in the middle of February. Your granny was completely deadpan. Here she was, "Herbie, stop playing with your Lego there. What do you say to your uncle Robin?"'

'Did I ever meet him?'

'Oh, no, he was long dead by the time you were born. Tragic really.'

'I think I can guess...'

'Well, I don't remember ever hearing the term then, but looking back I'd say it was Early Onset Alzheimer's.'

'That's a relief. I thought for a minute you were going to tell me it was Troublesitis.'

He wished he could have said he shared her relief. At least they seemed to have found a cure for Troublesitis, or the most virulent strain of it at any rate.

(Paul could testify to the persistence of a milder, but occasionally still just as dangerous strain.)

He wondered about those moments of profound detachment he had been experiencing in recent months. Was that how it began, the other thing? Was that how it began for Robin? There must have been a boy Robin once, teen too, a whole host of Robins, even eventually the Brut bringer, looking at him blankly from shore as the ship finally slipped its moorings. Drifted. Rudderless.

'I don't suppose you've any Baileys?' she said.

First drink they had ever let her have, when she was – fourteen? Younger? – this time of year too probably. 'Tastes like melted rum-and-raisin ice cream. I love it.'

He told her to check the top shelf of the cupboard next to the fridge. She did, and he had, Bushmills too, pushed right to the back, behind the other things he had no real use for these days, beater attachments, birthday candles, methylated spirits. She held the bottle up, angled, to the kitchen light. 'Enough for about two eggcupfuls, I'd say.'

'You can have mine.'

'That would defeat the whole purpose: it's a toast! Besides I don't think I could stomach more than a single eggcup any more.'

They toasted the wreath, the season, and that was their glasses pretty much drained.

A couple of evenings later, there was a knock at the door.

Herbie opened it to two men he had never seen before. Thirties. The haircut of the moment. A Canada goose emblem on the shoulder of one jacket, a cord collar on the waxed body of the other. It was cord-collar man who spoke.

'Nice wreath.'

'Nice of you to knock to tell me,' said Herbie. He was already halfway to what was coming next.

'We're from the Christians All Together Church.'

'I'm not really interested.'

A tilt of the head. 'In what?'

'Whatever it is you have come here to say.'

'Apart from the compliment about the wreath, you mean.'

'I'm even slightly sorry you said that now.'

The man pulled a little sideways smile. 'Would it surprise you if I told you I was as defensive as you are the first time someone from the church turned up on my doorstep?'

Herbie understood what was happening here, classic hustler's technique, draw the mark into a conversation, don't let him disengage. Understood, but couldn't stop himself. 'I'm not being defensive, I just want to get on with my evening.'

'I said life.'

'I'm sorry?'

'I asked the person who turned up on my doorstep to leave me to get on with my life. Although' – there was the sideways smile again – 'I may not have put it quite so politely.'

'I can vouch for that.' The Canada goose man spoke for the first time. He might actually have been Canadian. North American at any rate. 'It was me called at his door.'

The first man nodded. 'And, do you know what? Before the night was out, the pair of us were kneeling together right there in my hallway.'

He pointed past Herbie as though it had been right there in his.

Herbie looked from one expectant face to the other, then slowly sank down on to his knees, hands joined in supplication beneath his nose. 'Please, please, please,' he said, three taps of the hands against his chin and top lip, 'will the two of you turn around this minute and walk down my path?'

And with a shake of the head that suggested they knew better – would always know better – that was what they did.

'And shut the gate after you.'

They did that too. Or cord collar did. Left a hand on it a moment. 'We'll pray for you.'

'Whatever makes you happy,' Herbie said, because he was damned if he was going to let them have the last word. Damned too if he was going to have them still standing at the gate staring when he tried – *son of a bitch* – to get up off his knees.

Louise had mentioned on one of their early dates that she had gone away the past few years over Christmas and New

Year, skiing in Slovenia. She preferred to use her annual leave then, she told him, cut down on the opportunities the season provided for sitting and thinking what an utter car crash her life had turned into.

'Until you met me.'

'Goes without saying.'

One early December afternoon as she got up from his bed to get ready for her two-to-ten shift, he asked her if she would like to spend this Christmas with him and Beth.

She turned. 'Have you talked this through with Beth?'

'Well, she asked me what you normally did.' (She didn't. Didn't talk about Louise much at all.) 'You could just come for part of it, skip dinner, join us later for turkey sandwiches, or just go for a walk.'

She looked down the length of her face at her chest. She had missed a button. 'Attractive though that sounds' – there, that was it fixed – 'I think I am going to throw in my lot one more time with the Skingletons down in the Julian Alps. After some of the states they've seen me in, I feel I owe them at least that.'

'That's not really what yous call yourselves, is it?'

'Skingletons? More like they and themselves, but, yes, I'm afraid it is.'

'Do you think that might be part of their problem right there?'

She launched herself back on to the bed beside him, fingers seeking out his armpits. 'Listen to you, doling out relationship advice!'

He writhed, curled into a ball, fended her off with a pillow, play-bellowed finally and jack-knifed forward, but she was out the door and down the stairs before he had set so much as a foot on the ground.

They had their own mini Christmas the night before the night before she left. (An early morning flight out of Dublin; she didn't want to be cutting short the time they had or to spend it worrying about not waking up for the 4.30 Air Coach.) They went to a new rooftop hotel bar where, by Herbie's reckoning, they added between them five years to the average age of the few dozen revellers already installed. They mooched about by the doors on to the narrow, wall-length balcony – the very thing, seen from the street, that had enticed them in – until a table came free. It meant having to keep their coats on, even with the patio heaters planted every three or four feet going full blast. The view was over a high corrugated fence painted grey with black and red diagonal flashes, into a former police barracks. Or a former police barracks in the process of becoming a modern police station. 'You know,' she said, 'for the longest time I had no idea what was actually in there. I used to think from the fence it was a DIY store.'

'That reminds me of the graffiti: Help the RUC...'

'Beat yourself up! Even my old fella laughed at that one and he was the type would have got up and switched off the TV if there was somebody on it complaining about police brutality.'

'The famous Belfast black humour... Wouldn't you just have liked to grow up in a po-faced place with no bombs instead of one that prided itself on the speed with which it turned a tragedy into a gag?'

To the left a hundred yards, the Albert Clock offered them two of its four moon faces. The Cave Hill jutting out in black profile against the navy-blue sky was a head thrown back in silent howl. The clock hands went from downturned moustaches to evil villain eyebrows in the time it took them to finish off the bottle of wine they had ordered without realising how little appetite they had for it. Sheer bloody-minded Protestantism got them through it in the end. We're not paying that sort of money just to leave half of it sitting there!

They were on their last glass – shoulder to shoulder, and hand in hand beneath the table – when she reached sideways into her bag for a package, at more or less the same moment as he produced one from his overcoat pocket.

'Ha!' they said in unison.

They sat a moment, comparing wrapping paper and techniques. (Hers was nicer, his was neater.) 'Save for Christmas Day?' he said.

'Fuck that.'

'One, two, three…'

They unwrapped, he a book about walking along the border, she… a book about walking along the border. 'Well, what do you know about that?' she said. It wasn't as if it was even something they had ever talked about. 'Curious to say the least,' he said.

'I heard it…'

'On the radio…'

'And I thought…'

'Me too.'

As they descended in the lift at the end of their night, he wondered aloud whether the upstairs bar would slowly detach itself and float away without the ballast of their extra years to weight it down.

'It did OK before we got there,' she said. 'Anyway, some of those faces in there I don't think would bear too much scrutiny.'

Between the wine, the season, the prospect of not seeing one another for more than a fortnight, they thought about venturing down into the underpass just along from the hotel's entrance for a more than goodnight kiss but caught themselves on in the nick of time and wrapped their arms around one another where they stood on the footpath, mouths meeting… almost. Her hand came round from behind his back, stopping him short.

'Ahm, how do I say this? Your softback's digging into me.'

Shit. His overcoat pocket. He pulled the book out, bending back the cover in the process, revealing the inscription: his handwriting, his sweated-over, fretted-over words. 'Actually this one's yours… Sorry.'

She took it with her left hand and with her right gave him the one with the looping *Love Louise* on the flyleaf, the single *x*. She smoothed out the crease. Sort of. 'At least now we'll be able to tell them apart the moment we lift them down from the shelf.'

She looked him in the eye as she said it, then put her arms around his neck again the way she did the first time they kissed. It was something of a signature move and every bit as beguiling now as it was then. More, maybe. Yes, more. Everything was more. The word seemed to expand until it filled his entire being, in his head, in his mouth, in his hands on her waist.

When she unlocked her own hands its first letter was still on his lips. Mmmm.

'Is that going to do us, do you think, until I get back?'

'It'll just have to.'

He and Beth rose early on Christmas Eve morning and caught the bus into town. The lower deck couldn't have been more than a third full and when they walked upstairs to see if the front window seats were free, they found the top deck completely empty.

Maybe another bus had gone by, full, just before they arrived at the stop. Or maybe once again the whole festive season had peaked a little early.

The Christmas market had been taken down and packed away the afternoon before, all its churros and Schwenkgrilles and zoo burgers, its galettes and glühwein, its scented candles and hand-tooled leather, gone, leaving nothing for yards on end around the tree in the grounds of the City Hall but a muddy mess, Whoville after the Grinch had been. The shop windows along Donegall Place, running away from the City

Hall's front gates, had their sales signs up – some of them had never taken them down – and there was a general air of a second Sunday in the month (April, going by the weather), money all spent, and energy with it. Then cutting through it all came the sound of a violin, amplified by a horn attachment, at once louder and thinner, but playing 'Once in Royal David's City', and it came back to him that this had always been his favourite part of Christmas, ticking off the last things on the to-do list, knowing that after this it was home, the front door closed not to be opened again until Boxing Day. And maybe after all that was why the bus had been so empty: the turning inwards already underway.

He emptied his pockets of coins as he passed the violin player and dropped them into his open case. The man nodded, smiled. Beth apologised, trying to convey by hand gestures alone that she had to hold on to her money this morning. The man nodded again, smiled again, played on regardless.

A little further on, where Royal Avenue kinked across North Street, and where there were still the vestigial remains of the Seventies' Ring of Steel the last time he and Beth had done this, a long vista of building works opened up – a new campus for the University of Ulster, and hundreds of studio flats for the students who would attend it. The city was about to take a Great Leap Northwards into places he suspected he would never live to experience fully. He and Beth, though, turned east, at what his own father had taught him to call Blitz Square, on to Donegall Street – the old newspaper street, now, in its upper reaches, two long lines of restaurant and bar signs. A different place entirely. The cathedral at this lower end and the Dean standing on the kerb before it were almost the only constants, or – since this current Dean was the fourth or fifth descendant of the original Black Santa – the Dean's cape was, as though that was where the power was invested and the human beings took turns holding it up for a while.

The bishop from the Catholic cathedral on the west side of the Royal Avenue junction was keeping him company this morning. There was something in their various scarves and snoods and gloves over gloves that suggested the make-do of the trenches. Foot soldiers both in a war that showed no sign of ending. It was the bishop who lifted the lid for Beth to place her money in the wooden collecting barrel, standing, where a brazier might have, between them.

'God bless you,' the Dean said and reinforced the sentiment with a raised right hand.

'Merry Christmas,' Beth and Herbie chimed.

Beth took his arm as they walked away, up Donegall Street towards the old Assembly Rooms, snuggling up close. 'I never told you,' she said, when they were well out of earshot, 'but he used to terrify me.'

'Black Santa? But, wait, you asked to come, and you always seemed so happy.'

'Yeah, afterwards: tribute to the troll to ward off evil for another year.'

'So nothing to do with charity?'

'Oh, that too, that first probably, but you know how kids turn every little thing into good and bad juju. I was more scared of what would have happened if I had missed.'

A beer bike went across the end of the street. Santa hats, Weiss beer and women's voices Wizzarding.

Despite the sales there too, Christmas was still going strong round in the artfully deconstructed shopping centre that was Victoria Square, to where, describing an almost complete circle from (or was it to?) their bus stop, they wound their way next. They leaned on the mezzanine rail and looked down at a primary-school children's choir ranged before the flawless (because entirely artificial) Christmas tree, singing about bells ringing and other children singing and all being merry and bright.

'Are you going to hang a sock on the fireplace?' Herbie asked, taking his lead from the song, and thinking of the big multicoloured stripy thing she had had when she was small, the toe reaching almost to the hearth, and the neck – when they held it up against her – to the tip of her nose.

'I might just.'

They wandered through a while, not talking much, not buying anything, barely even looking. It was the crowd they craved, the sense of common purpose, which was simply to be there, finally. They decided on hot ports (the second drink he and Tanya had let her have) in the Kitchen Bar, somewhere not a hundred miles from where the old Kitchen Bar used to be. He had met Alice Clark there one Saturday afternoon, the autumn after the summer trip they had started together and ended apart. She apologised for leaving him high and dry like that. She hardly knew herself what had come over her, other than that she was far from home, and all sense of right and wrong, and, well, the guy had turned out to be a shit – slept with her friend from Guides as well – but even if he hadn't, she would have regretted it. Did regret it. Herbie had been her first, and she knew she had been his, and that had to mean something, hadn't it?

And he had had to say to her, it's too late, Alice. Much, much, much too late.

In America, heading up her own law firm, last he heard.

'OK,' Beth said when she had squeezed the last of the port from her lemon with the heel of the spoon and drunk it down, 'now we're ready.'

She didn't hang up a sock in the end. He put a few small things in a pillowcase and hung it on her door handle, the way they had started to do once she hit her teens. Chocolates, a novel, the DVD of a film she had complained had dropped off Netflix.

She had already accepted, grudgingly and with embarrassment, that her big present was going to be invisible, an electronic money transfer.

She gave him – oh very funny – a bottle of Brut at breakfast the next morning, then, just long enough after that he had begun to wonder (though he understood, of course he did), passed him a long, pale blue envelope, containing...

'A fixture list.'

'I couldn't quite run to a season ticket, even there, and anyway it's half over, but they said if you just picked half a dozen you fancied…' Her voice tailing away. 'You seemed to get such a kick out of it last time you went.'

'I did,' he said. 'I'd been meaning to get back.'

She sat forward then. 'They were saying that when I went in to buy it. Soon as I said your name, here they all were, "Ach, sure tell Herbie to just turn up on the days, we'll look after him."'

And there was one other thing. She stood and cleared her throat and recited – with only a couple of glances down at the text on her phone – Leigh Hunt's Christmas poem: 'What! do they suppose that every thing has been said that *can* be said about any one Christmas thing?', followed by a long list of many an early 1800s Christmas thing about which you could never say enough (hackins, Julklaps and wad-shooting being three of the more dubious, saluting the apple trees one of the more surreal), culminating in the greatest plum pudding for the greatest number…

Beth by way of full stop, and for want of the thing itself, bit into another mince pie – the twenty-fifth of Christmas – and immediately clutched her stomach.

'I don't think I'm going to be able to eat my dinner before midnight.'

Tanya Skyped later in the morning from Bali, where it was already Christmas night. The fairy lights behind her swayed in the sea breeze. She and Martin – he was somewhere offscreen – appeared to have spent the eight hours' time difference drinking sparkling Shiraz. 'Don't knock it till you've tried it, *lots*,' she said and collapsed sideways in a fit of giggles, till Martin's hand, or its extended forefinger, entered the frame and righted her... for twenty seconds... until she toppled out the other side.

'Wow, I've never seen her so pissed,' Beth said when they had rung off. 'Or so...'

'Happy?'

'At one with herself.'

He was going to ask her if there was a difference, but it would have sounded like he was taking issue with her general point, and really there was no arguing with that.

Beth, in matters of Christmas at least, a believer in the physical object, had insisted too on buying cards. The day before Christmas Eve he went up and down the street pushing envelopes through letterboxes where there was no one at home, knocking if he saw a light. 'Just wanted to say Happy Christmas – no, not stopping...' He wound up at the gate of the house directly opposite, Audrey Bannon's. He nearly didn't bother, but, ah, what the heck. He walked up the path – thought as he reached the door he could hear a TV somewhere in the rear, or maybe from upstairs. He knocked. Waited. Nothing. As expected. He pushed the card through the letterbox anyway, with best wishes for Christmas and the New Year. 'I doubt you'll thank me for it,' he muttered as he closed the gate behind him.

So it was one of the bigger surprises that Christmas Day when, just after darkness fell, he heard the kitten mewl of his own letterbox rising and falling and pulled back the curtain to find a card lying on the hall floor. 'Herbie and Daughter' it said on the front. She had put the house number in brackets after her signature.

'Do you think she was worried you wouldn't know who she was without it?' Beth asked.

'I think maybe she is finally starting to admit to herself she lives there.'

They cleared the table after their late, late dinner and played a board game. Or read the rules and tried to set a board game up. It was like someone had torn a novel apart and shuffled the pages. *Finnegans Wake*, maybe. Then asked you to roll a double six to see them. One at a time. Actually it was like one of the games he remembered Beth playing with her friends when she was small, which were all scene-setting and name-choosing and deciding how the parents had died – because the parents, it was agreed without it ever having to be said, *had* to be dead – and then – 'Beth! your tea's ready!' – everything put on hold until tomorrow when the names and scenes and causes of death would be debated all over again.

In place of the call to tea tonight was the sound of a message arriving on Beth's phone.

'Aw, that's so nice of her.' She turned the phone so he could see the message. He recognised the sender – which is to say the Receiver – by the Old Geezer emoji. 'Taking time out of her Christmas Day like that.'

He did think about asking whether that might be considered

to be going above and beyond, just a touch... But he held his tongue: some people were just nice.

Beth texted back. Got another in return. That happened two or three times more. The board game was quietly forgotten.

He finished the day as he had begun it, with a rapid back and forth of texts of his own with Louise. A quiet Christmas she had had. Exactly as she had wanted it. A walk along the lake shore, lunch with her friends, a couple of glasses of wine. There was a party just starting, but she wasn't going to go to it. 'I never do,' she added.

'I'm going to read my book now,' he wrote at last.

'Me too. Think of me, I'll think of you.'

He read as far as page two and awoke in the wee small frozen hours with it open on his chest. He set it on the floor beside his bed. The border would still be there in the morning.

It was there six mornings later, thirty pages or so further traversed, when he opened his eyes on New Year's Day.

His resolution that year as every year, made as he lay in bed waiting for his alarm, was do less, better.

The 'less' he felt he had maybe made some headway on. One of these years he would get to grips with the 'better'.

One of these years he would learn how to focus on a single task to the exclusion of all others, work out finally what he was all about. He turned on to his back and listened to his breathing, the long slow in and accelerating out of it. Wouldn't it be funny if that was what it turned out to be? The ultimate point of him. Keep doing that… i-i-i-i-n andout, i-i-i-i-n andout, i-i-i-i-n andout, i-i-i-i-n and

Stop.

Alarm.

Go.

Twenty-eighteen.

9

Sam and Derek had heeded their solicitor's advice and rented a place up the North Antrim coast where at nights they sat before the open fire, tumblers of whiskey in hand, and plotted their reopening. As the weeks dragged on and the cost of the trade lost mounted, their plans were scaled back, from glitzy to grand, from grand to statement, from statement to Sam just walking up to the door in the end on the fourth morning of the year and turning the sign back the way it had been facing before Derek stepped into the yard ten weeks before and saw the rat.

Business that first week was slow. There was the inevitable Christmas hangover, of course, January pay cheques received a week early and already half spent. But they had to face the fact, too, a rat was a rat, however it got there, and the memory of it was going to be ten times harder to erase than the physical trace.

At least the Post Office staff returned, walked across the road, each at his or her designated tea break time, and pushed open the door as though it had never been shut at all. Sam and Derek at the counter.

'The usual?'

'The usual.'

Herbie was in there before any of them for his own usual. He met Neeta as he was settling up with Derek.

'How are things across there?' Derek asked her.

'Starting to run the stock down now we've Christmas out of the way,' she said, although every time Herbie had been in there in the lead-up there had seemed to be more bare shelves than there were actual goods for sale.

'Including the greetings cards?' he asked.

'Oh dear God, no,' Neeta said. 'Those things will never shift. I swear, some of them must predate me.'

The postmaster had told her and the rest of the staff before the holiday not to expect to see him more than a couple of times a week once they got back. He would be spending most of his days from here on in briefing his successor in the filling station half a mile away.

'Is that still the word for it, do you think?' Neeta asked. 'I mean, they already have a bakery, a butcher, a dry-cleaner's and a greengrocer in there. And now a Post Office counter?'

If it went on like this there would just be them and the CATCH left. God versus Big Oil. And a load of little cafes and charity shops in between fighting for the scraps.

'I remember I used to think it was great when that filling station started doing peanuts beside the till,' Neeta said. 'I never dreamed they would end up swallowing up everything else.'

'Well, I suppose they're seeds, aren't they, peanuts?' Derek said. 'It all grows from there.'

The people working in it were sound, Neeta was quick to add, couldn't be more apologetic any time she was in, sure they had used that Post Office themselves from when they were no age – first savings accounts, premium bonds, cashing grandparents' postal orders. (Yeah, but did you ever buy a card?) Say, though, she was, I don't know – eighty-five; say she didn't have a car; say even walking to the shops was getting hard for her, was she really going to fancy taking her chances on that forecourt, those big four-wheel-drive things people drove now? She didn't think so. Mind you, she wasn't so sure she would fancy it either going in there on a Monday morning with a carrier bag full of cash, trying to pick her way through the people queuing for the baker, the butcher, the greengrocer... the dry-cleaner.

'You're not telling us,' said Herbie, 'you think you are an easy touch over there?'

'I prefer "more straightforward proposition": it's a square box of a room with a door in one wall and a counter facing. No nasty surprises lurking, no clients under the age of seventy most of the time who could pounce the minute your back is turned.'

'I suppose it's like any other line of work, you have to ensure the smoothest possible running. I mean they have their materials – shopkeepers, amusement arcade owners, what have you – they have their particular set of tools…'

'Which they don't even have to use, just the thought that they have them at all is enough. That's probably the best tool in the whole kit.'

'Probably, and off they go every day…'

'And night…'

'… to extract maximum value from their materials, see that it's safely deposited.'

'I suppose when you put it like that. You'd nearly want to put your hand in your own pocket.'

'If one of theirs wasn't there first.'

They were so caught up in their little three-way riff they had none of them clocked the door opening.

'You know if they even heard you talking like that, they would shove a pipe bomb through your letterbox?'

They all looked round at the same time. Paul.

With a stick.

He used it to turn a seat towards him, table nearest the door, and sat down into it. 'The usual,' he said. 'Thanks.'

'Jesus, Paul, is that still from your accident?'

'Depends which accident you're talking about.'

'Don't tell me you've had another one?'

He shook his head. 'See this place?' he said.

A couple of weeks before Christmas Paul had collected an enormous order of pizzas for delivery to a house where there was a party going on: fifteen monster deep-pan meat feasts and a dozen garlic pizza breads with cheese; over £250 worth. Took him ten minutes getting them in the boot at one end of the journey and out again at the other end, an ordinary-looking semi-detached, from which a truly frightening squall of music was coming. 'I've been at quieter festivals,' he said.

Some wee squirt came to the door, couldn't have been more than sixteen, jumper on him saying 'Do my baubles look big in this?', huge big lovebite on his neck, and insisted on carrying the whole lot in in one go – he could hardly see over the top once the garlic breads were added, but he turned around anyway and then didn't he try to close the door with his foot. Paul stuck his own foot in to stop him. 'It's not paid for yet,' he said and the squirt twisted his head as far as it would go without causing a garlic bread avalanche and told him to fuck right off, which with hindsight (and possibly even fore-) Paul would have been well advised to do, because the next thing, when he said he wasn't budging, this big fucker – 'Pull my cracker', his jumper said, with an arrow pointing down – came barrelling out of the kitchen – Paul could see gleeful faces, women's and men's, in the doorway – and down the hall towards him. Here he was, 'Nobody tell you, mate? We don't pay.' And then he stopped. 'Fuck me, it's you.'

It was him, the guy – the brigadier – who had driven into Paul's Uber car. He started to laugh, put a big hand on Paul's shoulder. 'You're really not having a good run of it, are you?' he said, pat, pat, pat then *push* – out the door Paul went, staggering backwards, off the front step, over the garden kerb, losing his balance completely and landing – *shit and fuck* – tailbone on crazy paving, next to a landlocked camellia.

He sat for half an hour outside the pizza place before he was able to turn far enough in his seat to open the car door.

And what did they do? Docked him five nights' pay. Here was the manager to him, 'You're not supposed to leave the client's premises without payment, no exceptions.'

Paul asked her if she would like to go round there and try and get the money herself. 'Not my job,' she said, 'and not my concern. My job – my only concern – is to make sure the books balance at the end of every week and I can tell you here and now one way or another they will.'

When the call came in on New Year's Eve to take a delivery to a party at the same address, another couple of hundred quid's worth, Paul point-blank refused. (He had been using the stick since he took the tumble before Christmas but left it in the car any time he went in to do a pick-up in case the manager gave his shift to one of the other drivers.) When the manager said to him she wasn't *asking* him to do it, she was *telling* him, he started emptying his pockets on to the counter, pound coins, silver, a fiver folded over.

'Here was me to them,' he said, 'take it. I might as well pay you now as later.' He had the car keys out now too. 'You can take them while you're at it, that's me, finished.'

The manager shouted after him, 'You know I won't be able to give you a reference if you just walk out like this in the middle of your shift?'

'Like that's seriously going to affect my future prospects.'

'Any other time I would have told you you could have had a job in here,' Derek said, and set Paul's tea down before him, 'but the way things have been lately…'

Paul batted away the apology. 'Don't worry, I'll be all right,' he said. 'I've got a couple of things in mind.'

Neeta warned him to be careful. 'You know what they say about things happening in threes.' Paul assured her he was going to make absolutely certain not to bump into that guy again – or be bumped into by him – any time soon.

'That's maybe easier said than done,' said Neeta. 'Unless you're thinking of getting out of here altogether.' Paul stirred his tea. 'Aw, you're not, are you?'

The rain that had been threatening all morning chose that moment to unleash itself: 0–60 in two seconds flat.

'And miss all the lovely weather?' Paul said. 'Nah.'

Three hours into the rain, just about the point where it tipped into extreme weather event, Herbie texted Louise. 'Pity you arriving home to this.'

He was pretty sure it was today she got back. The last text he had had from her was eight o'clock on New Year's Eve. She was getting ready to head out with some of the others to watch the firework display. The networks were bound to be jammed come midnight, so she was getting her greetings in early.

He had thought nothing of it when he didn't hear from her the next day, hadn't dwelt too much on the fact that he didn't hear from her the day after that again, though he had sent her a couple of messages in the meantime, asking about her travel arrangements, hoping she had fun her last couple of days on the slopes.

The day after that again… '*Dad!*' Beth caught him at dinner, checking his phone under the table. 'That's about the tenth time since we sat down you've done that. What was it you used to say to me: why don't you just ring?'

He left it until later that night, then rang. Answer machine. 'Hi, this is Louise, I'd like to say I have something better to do than come to the phone, but it's probably just sitting, charging somewhere where I can't hear it. Tell me who you are and as soon as I have found it, I'll call you back.'

He told her he was Herbie. (How odd his own name had always sounded from his own mouth.) Then he waited.

After a couple of hours of that he began to wonder whether something had happened, whether, instead of charging, the phone was lying out of reach on a table next to a hospital bed at the foot of a Julian Alp, or worse, was within reach but useless to her heavily bandaged hands. Finally, he went on to her Facebook page. It felt like spying. But she definitely wasn't in hospital, and – a snapshot from her kitchen window of the previous day's rain marathon – she was definitely back in Belfast. The days passed, became a week.

She would be back at work now. He could just have walked round there and seen her. Except he couldn't.

The couple of times he found himself on the bus he couldn't bring himself even to get off at the stop across the car park, getting up from his seat a stop early the first time and, the next (scrupulously – strenuously – avoiding looking out the window as he passed), three stops late.

From there it was a long and many-side-streeted walk home. Due to the slight curve in his own street, and the direction from which, on this occasion, he approached it, he didn't see until he was quite some way down Louise standing before his front door, dressed in her work jerkin. He was another ten yards closer before she – turning away – caught sight of him. 'Have they got you on home deliveries now?' was all he could think to say.

She shook her head, her eyes closing, as though the shake was directed inward. Don't be deflected.

'Will you come in a minute?'

Eyes open, a nod.

He had to squeeze past her on his way to open the door, talking the while, inanely, he knew, though he was completely incapable of stopping, about the stiffness of the lock, about the new mat he had had to buy after the people-two-up's cat sprayed against the door seal...

'I'm sorry,' she said as soon as they were inside, 'I should have phoned you before now,' which was the easier of the two apologies she had come there to make.

She sank down on to the edge of the sofa. 'It's just, I don't really know how to explain this. I went out on New Year's Eve...'

And there was a guy, he thought, whatever the fifty-something equivalent was of a beat-up guitar slung across his back (unless it was, in fact, a beat-up guitar slung across his back). 'And it occurred to me,' she said, 'as I was standing, off by myself, watching this big firework display they had on, I didn't *miss* you the way I thought I was going to, the way I was hoping I would, and I like you, Herbie, I really, really do, but...' She opened her hands. 'Does that make sense?'

'No, no,' he said, meaning yes, 'of course, entirely.'

She stood up, deeper-than-sighed, closer to exorcism than exhalation. 'I hope this isn't going to make things awkward between us.'

'We'll not let it.'

He walked her to the door again, pulled it open.

And there was Beth, just about to put her key in the lock.

'Oh, hello, you must be Louise,' she said. 'How lovely to meet you properly at last.'

So not the best start to a future free from awkwardness.

'If it's any comfort,' Beth started to say when Louise had gone and he had explained what had just happened, but Herbie stopped her short.

'At the minute, I don't think, whatever it is, it's going to be.'

'Right.'

'Thank you all the same.'

'Right.'

It went on for days, the hurting.

He worked through it, going into the Records Office each morning, whether or (more often) not he had anything in particular of his own to do, trading the un-contracted four fifths of himself for the simple distraction of other people's lives, unfolding in the moment, or already played out, awaiting the handwritten request or emailed enquiry to pull them up out of the archive and set them running again.

He got to know Lidl a whole lot better too.

It was as though he was in fact constructing a bypass, not just in his routine but in his mind. There would still be roads into that bypassed-Herbie and the months (though funny already to think it was only months) he had spent with Louise, but he wouldn't take them any more, or when at last he did – by some unexpected detour – it would be to stand disoriented, struggling for connection or even recognition.

Like Dr Ross said: Toome.

Mind you, he kept the volume on his phone set to high any time he wasn't in the Records Office. Just in case.

Gradually, he let his hours slip back to their pre-Louise levels. Mid-afternoon would find him again as often as not sitting in the window of Sam's, the table under the capital S, contemplating his first and last coffee of the day.

Once or twice, seeing as he drew close that the table wasn't free, he had carried on by, as he would have the afternoon the three schoolgirls in bright blue blazers got to it before him, if Derek hadn't at that moment been setting their tray in front of them and seen him (the girls were too preoccupied with their phones to pay Derek any heed) through the glass.

Derek beckoned him in.

By the time Herbie arrived he was behind the counter, hand spread on the iPad. 'I see they are at it again,' he said. 'The dumpers: two hundred and fifty tyres in the Slievenacloy Nature Reserve.'

Not on the scale of a Portakabin on a mountain roadside, but the image that Derek turned towards him was still enough to make the heart sink.

'Unless, maybe, do you think they're starting early for the Eleventh Night?'

Not all that likely, to judge by the little map inserted in the bottom corner of the tyres image, locating the reserve in an area more Green, in Belfast electoral headcount speak, than Orange, though equally not all that early either. Herbie or the boy who shared his name had built his fair share of July bonfires. Window-shopping for hatchets began as soon as the boxes with the Christmas decorations in them were shouldered up through the black hole into the roof space. If you hadn't hacked the branches off a couple of saplings by the end of February you were lagging way behind. By Easter you would want to have constructed your hut out of the bits and pieces that you had scavenged or that the people roundabout had turfed out for you, there to sit and guard your ever-growing pile – containing, if you were lucky, a baldy tyre or two, or five at most, for the smoke effect – until the Eleventh Night.

Derek started humming – unknown quite possibly to himself – 'A Day in the Life'. Two-fifty tyres in Slieve-na-cloy-Re-serve.

(Now they know how many tyres it takes to burn the Albert Hall…)

'Comments from the councillors?' Herbie asked. If he'd had a waistcoat he'd have hooked his thumbs in it.

Derek swallowed the hum, stroked the screen. 'Let's see – ah! here it's here. Surprise, surprise: calling for a crackdown.' He frowned. 'No, wait… there *was* a crackdown, last year. Since when…' reading a bit more in silence, 'you'll not believe this' – meeting Herbie's eye then – 'the fly-tipping has gone up.'

It was like a game: the more you tell us we can't, the more we will.

'Death held no terror for them,' said Derek, hamming, 'or at least the eighty-pound fixed penalty notice held none. Eighty pound! You'd nearly pay that yourself not to have to sit and go through your recycling once in a while.' He turned so quickly to the coffee machine that he had it on before Herbie could say not to bother.

Herbie had been aware of the schoolgirls on the edge of his hearing all the time he was talking to Derek, getting themselves worked up about whatever it was they were looking at on their phones. Or on one of their phones, over which they were all leaning, two of them half out of their seats, pointing. Turned out – he caught sight as he passed with his coffee – not to be a phone at all but a calculator, an equation on its display that seemed to be the result of someone falling asleep headfirst on the keyboard.

'No, no, no,' one of the girls grabbed a copybook from the

table in front of her friend and started to write. 'Like *this*… See… It's a continuity equation.'

Herbie sat, two tables along, putting off the moment of that first sip, which inevitably hastened the last. It had not simply been a fit of pique at missing out on his favourite table that caused him to pass by – or at least attempt to – just now. That had only helped push to the forefront of his mind the things at home that needed doing. But now that he was sitting down, coffee before him, the urgency of those and all other things receded. And then – with a Ryanair-style fanfare – an SMS message found its way by means far beyond his comprehension into his trouser pocket, from… where? Who? – he fumbled to pull it out. Tanya.

He stuffed the phone away again. (That *was* pure pique.) A few moments later, more horns; one of the schoolgirls looked over her shoulder at him: *seriously?* And a few moments after that still more, and – even as he was retrieving it from his pocket a second time (all three of the girls turned his way by now) – even more. Tanya, Tanya, Tanya. She was writing a flipping essay.

Don't be alarmed, were the first words he read. The next word that jumped out was *chemo*.

The polyp on the lining of her womb, if he remembered? Turned out it was not quite so benign as the doctors had at first thought, although – again, don't be alarmed – they were still confident it was treatable, as was she. 'Well, you have to be, don't you?'

He looked at his cup as he closed the final text. Empty. He couldn't remember having lifted it once.

He rang the moment he was out the door.

'Oh, listen, you didn't have to,' Tanya said. Did her voice sound different? He thought of the cassette tapes he had grown up with, how with use and repeated taping over they would sometimes get stretched, and how no amount of tightening – fingertip jammed in the spool – could ever quite put them right.

She told him in her new stretched voice that she had known before Christmas, but that she hadn't wanted to say to anyone, not even Martin. What was the point of making everybody else's Christmas miserable? Besides, it had cost them an absolute fortune, the place they had booked in Bali. She was damned if she was just going to wave goodbye to that. She told him too all about the consultant. They had league tables for this kind of thing, survival-to-diagnosis ratios, and his were the highest – or was it the lowest? whichever was the best – in the whole of Ireland.

She had to stop after getting that all out to catch her breath.

'Oh, I'm not saying it's a picnic, any of it, but you know what they say, what doesn't kill you...' The words hung in the air a moment. 'That means it's *not* going to kill me, you know that, don't you. I just won't let it.'

He had been pacing up and down all this time outside the cafe. He saw the schoolgirls looking at him through the window, conscious maybe that they were in the presence of a problem that not even continuity equations perfectly executed could solve.

'But here,' Tanya said, 'I haven't said anything to Beth yet. You're there with her every day, I'll let you be the judge of when's the best time.'

He thought for all of two minutes before he decided there was no way in the message-saturated world he could keep the news from Beth now that Tanya had begun to let it out, even supposing there was a case to be made for should.

He walked from Sam's to the former lemonade bottling plant, by way of tree-lined avenue and tight-terraced street, strung-out ribbon development and nucleated cluster (any given mile of any given city was a potted history of ideas about what that city ought to be), coaching himself all the while in what to say and how to say it. There was a lot of shoulder work involved, twitches, shrugs, rolls.

He came out eventually on to a wide road on the far side of which he walked through an archway into a yard full of facilities vans and catering vans and dressing-room trailers and four-wheel-drives with privacy windows and, the runt of this motley litter, a claret-coloured Smart car with the New Eyes NI name in china blue.

A security guard watched from behind a sliding door as he turned about in the middle of the yard trying to get his bearings, then just as the guard took a step towards his door, Beth came out of another on the far side of the yard, chatting to a girl in a boiler suit and bowler hat, who seemed to intuit – before Beth had even clocked him – a connection between her and Herbie, and nothing but ill from his being there. Beth, alerted by her friend's hesitation, turned towards him. Her face at the sight of him lit up, and the second after darkened. 'Has Louise…?'

He shook his head: nothing to do with her.

'It's not Paul again, is it?'

'I just had a long chat with your mum,' he managed at last, and she said, 'Oh, crap.'

The girl with the bowler hat laid a hand lightly on Beth's shoulder before withdrawing again into the building.

The security guard sat at his counter again and took out his phone.

'She's dying, isn't she?' Beth said.

'Not if she has anything to do with it.'

He filled her in as they walked, her arm in his. The consultant was saying six to eight sessions of chemo ought to do the job. Very matter of fact. People went through this every day. He couldn't walk down a street in all of Munster without bumping into someone who had had exactly the same treatment she was going to have, and you would never know to look at them they had ever had a thing wrong with them. She had already had her first session and was feeling predictably shit, but she was staying positive.

'I'm going to go down there,' Beth said when he had finished.

'Don't you have to stay in the UK?'

'Where did you hear that? Anyway, it's not as if I have to apply for a visa, I'm just jumping on the bus.'

He wanted to tell her some of the stories he had heard the last while, of immigration spot checks along the main road south of the border, of passengers being taken off and driven to the Garda station in Dundalk for questioning, but stories for now was all they were, passed on always by the friend of a friend of the person who had witnessed them. And with the news she had had this afternoon she didn't need anything else to worry her.

He on the other hand did need, while it was fresh in his mind again, to call into the Post Office and pick up an Irish passport renewal form.

They had arrived at the traffic lights just down from M&S.

'How are we off for stuff for dinner?' she said. 'I don't mind taking a run in.'

'No,' he said and pressed her arm to his side, 'we'll be fine.'

Beth rang Roza first thing next morning and explained she was going to have to take a couple of weeks off. Roza said if she remembered to look out the bus window now and then they could mark part of it down as a work trip. Meantime Beth wasn't to worry about Micky and her, they would get on to one of the agencies straight away.

'I suggested she give Paul a ring,' Beth told Herbie, as they sat on the bus together into town.

'Do you think he'd do it?'

'I don't know, I texted him last night to give him a heads-up. He told me he was waiting on something else coming through. I'll call and see him when I get back.'

He accompanied her as far as the Air Coach stop up the side of the Opera House. She phoned him eleven hours later to say she had arrived. It really was the other end of the island. She sounded as though she was in the middle of a hurricane. 'I had to walk down the garden,' she said. 'The signal's all over the place indoors. And also' – hand cupped over her mouth for added effect – 'it's all too weird in there. I mean Martin's a lovely guy, dotes on Mum, but he's like a child. She's worried his anxiety over her is making him sick – she actually said that – so she's running around doing things for him and her hair is coming out in clumps…' She paused. 'Ah, come on,' she said then, at the very end of patience.

'What is it?'

'He's playing his guitar again. Must be the tenth time since I got here. Mum says it's his way of relieving stress – passing it on, more like. Listen…' All Herbie could hear at first was wind – all the winds of the world it might have been – but then he caught something at the back of it. Stray notes from far down the neck. He wanted to say 'Whiskey in the Jar'. Beth came back on. 'Desperate, isn't it?' He actually didn't think it sounded too bad. 'I'd better go back in,' she said, but whatever way she did it she didn't hang up properly and for the next half a minute he was treated to her exaggeratedly heavy footfall, the wild west Cork wind and his ex-wife's lover's painstaking guitar solo. For the first time since he got Tanya's text – in longer, in fact, than he could remember – he cried, actual sobs that caught in his throat.

'Are you still there?' Beth asked, as though it was his doing. And without waiting for an answer banished him completely.

It took a couple of days, but she came round to Martin by and by. Despite the repeated ambition-trumping-ability guitar stylings. And the conspiracy theories. Theory. The Big They. Out to get you one way or another and to thwart or take down anything that held out the promise of a Martin-ordered world, which as best as Beth could sum it up was Socialism Without Tinkers – he would not be dissuaded from describing Travellers as such nor see their exclusion as incompatible with his professed egalitarianism.

'I will not take lectures from anyone. I have lived at close quarters with these people and believe me I know what I am talking about.'

'His mother had a very bad experience,' Tanya said as though that settled the matter. Martin often backed up his opinions (and Tanya endorsed them) with examples of things that had befallen or, occasionally, benefited members of his family, of which there appeared to be a good many. Like saints, nearly, or ancient gods, each with their own area of special interest, from sewers to oceans and even (Cousin Janice) bi-fold aluminium patio doors.

Tanya looked on him, Beth thought, with a mixture of

bemusement and barely contained desire. 'I honestly think she could eat him if she thought she'd have as much left when she finished as she had when she began.'

Just don't try talking to him about illness. 'He has too good a heart,' was Tanya's explanation. 'The thought of anyone suffering is nearly too much for him.'

He didn't need asking twice then when Beth offered to go with Tanya to an appointment with the consultant in Cork. Beth had to go outside and be by herself for a while, the night before, after she saw Tanya's carefully chosen outfit for the day on a hanger in the utility room: navy double-breasted blazer, white-and-lemon-striped blouse, white culottes, new knickers and bra.

Tanya herself did the driving, one of those black sport utility vehicles that Beth had always found ridiculous (Belfast at rush hour she said looked like one big presidential motorcade), but that did, she had to acknowledge, have a kind of logic in the rocky roads around Schull.

Beth saw them reflected in the occasional glances of passing motorists (a good half of them in SUVs too, so on their eye level). A mother and daughter, chatting and laughing, on their way up to the city for nothing more pressing than lunch or maybe a spot of shopping. Even when they arrived at the hospital you would have been hard put, she thought, to tell that Tanya was a patient, not a visitor or even a benefactor. She wanted to show Beth everything, as though she had paid for it all. ('She's paying for more of it than she would be up here,' said Herbie.)

The consultant was held up on his way from another appointment (heavy helicopter traffic coming in from Waterford; so much for him walking down any street in Cork), meaning they ended up in the waiting room for about half an hour. Though they were well looked after – pampered, Beth would almost have said – that was the only time Beth saw her mother scared. 'You tell yourself you're reconciled to the fact of dying,' Tanya said to Beth twenty-odd minutes into the wait, 'but of course you aren't at all. It's not some hazy fade-out, it's a ruddy great wall and sooner or later you're going to hit it. I just want it to be later. Much, much later.'

The consultant, however, when he did arrive, was very upbeat – very windswept-looking *and* upbeat. (He piloted the helicopter himself, apparently with the window open.)

He talked them through the most recent scans. ('They must have been Ultra HD', Beth said. 'I felt like I was right inside there, which was confusing to say the least.') There was already a marked shrinkage in the size of the tumour – the kind of thing you might expect to see after four or five months rather than four or five weeks. Even so Tanya was subdued in the car back to Schull, Beth now taking over the driving. (She would defy any cop or court that tried to fine or prosecute her.) She had seemed to be half asleep, in fact, head resting against the window, when she suddenly opened her eyes and announced she wanted to be buried at home. That was good to know, Beth told her, but it wasn't going to be happening any time soon.

'I am sure you're right. Even so, it needs to be said. I can't talk to Martin about it. It would only upset him.' She rested her head on the window again. 'He has too good a heart,' she said quietly.

She did sleep then, didn't wake until the car was turning off the lane into the driveway. She pulled down the sun visor before getting out of the car, checking her face in the mirror for streaks. She turned to Beth and asked her not to judge her, or Martin. Beth leaned across and put her arms around her, said she wasn't in a position to judge anyone.

'I think she is going to come through this OK,' she told Herbie at the conclusion of her exhaustive account. 'And I think she is in the place she needs to be, now and always.'

She had started to leave the room when she remembered something and turned back and sat on the arm of the sofa. 'I never told you, the day I was travelling down, just before the bus pulled out these two girls got on and went straight back down to the bottom of the bus, looked like they were going to a gig or a party, no luggage apart from a carry-out, which they'd obviously started in on already, half ten in the morning – completely plastered the both of them, in a giggly, everybody's my best friend way. They were all like, *aw*, and, *that's so sweet*. We were barely out of the city centre when one of them announced she needed to pee, so of course next thing her friend needs to go too, and they start talking about where the bus pulls in…'

'I thought the Air Coach was an Express?' said Herbie.

'Exactly. We passed the exit sign for Sprucefield and this

one gave a wee yelp, Oh, Janey, it's not stopping! And some man across the aisle – nice guy – he told them the first stop was Dublin Airport. And here they were, *Dublin Airport?* We can't hang on till Dublin Airport. Well, that was them from then on, all they talked about was how badly they needed to go, *swear to God*… if I heard that once I heard it a hundred times. Swear to God, I can't hold on much longer… Swear to God, I am going to pee all over this floor. And the moans of them! The driver shouted down the bus at them to stay in their seats because they were pacing up and down the aisle, the pair of them.'

'They really should have toilets,' said Herbie, seeing it from their point of view.

'They should, but anyway, there they were, no toilet, and no hope of one for another eighty or ninety miles. I was going to say they had everybody's heads turned, but you know what people are like in those situations, they would look anywhere but at what is actually going on, and then all of a sudden – we must have been driving for an hour and a half by this stage – the bus started slowing down and they were crouching, leaning across people, looking out the window, and here's one of them, Look, look, it's the border, we'll have to stop! And they flew up to the front of the bus and started badgering the driver. Will you let us off here over by that bit of wall…'

Herbie said, 'A wall? At the border? What road were you on?'

'The M1. But that's the thing, it wasn't the border at all, it was the Toll Plaza.'

'Drogheda?' About thirty miles into the Irish Republic. 'They didn't seriously think…'

'I suppose they just saw the barriers and thought, you know: frontier!'

'I know the wall now. More like a sculpture?'

'Like a big public toilet to them.'

'Did the driver let them off?'

'One of them had her jeans half down, he'd no choice. I'm not kidding you, you could hear them even over the sound of all those cars and lorries revving their engines – the sighs of them from the other side of that wall… And their faces when they got back on, you'd think they had won a prize fight.'

She did a little shimmy with her shoulders, fists pumping.

Herbie said, 'I like the fact that they thought you had to pay to get over the border.'

'I like the fact that they thought they were having a wee-wee on it. Talk about marking your territory. And the fact that they started again as soon as they were back in their seats, beating into the carry-out.'

'That's dedication.'

'And actually, when you think about it, real self-control. I mean they knew when to stop as well as start, and they did hold it in.'

Later that night, lying in bed, grasping for sleep, he found his thoughts turning to the spring of the year after he started secondary school. Three Scottish soldiers went for a drink in

a bar downtown one early March Saturday night, brothers
two of them, one of them not even old enough to drink. They
met some men there who told them about a party they were
going to, asked them if they fancied coming along. It was a
bit of a drive, like, but sure they could bring their pints with
them, and there'd be girls there, more than enough to go
round. So, yeah, the three boys said, why not, and out they
went and got into the men's car, and it was a drive, all right,
they had to ask the driver to stop in the end to let them get
out and take a leak. They were up in the hills above the city –
the Hightown Road. However they had managed it, they were
still holding on to their pint glasses, even as they were lining
up at the side of the road to do the business. One of the men
who had been in the car with them, chatting and carrying on
the whole way up the road, got out with a gun in his hand and
walked along behind them and shot two of them in the back
of the head. When the third one turned the gunman shot him
in the chest. Then he got back into the car with his mates and
drove away, leaving three bodies there like so much refuse.

The soldiers' faces for days afterwards were on all the
front pages and news bulletins, smiling out from under the
regimental caps with the tartan trim and black satin ribbon
hanging down at the back.

Boys where Herbie lived started wearing tartan scarves
in memory of them, knotted round their wrists rather than
round their necks. Other – Protestant – boys in other parts
of the city were doing the same. A virus to which all other
sections of the population were immune. You could tell when

you saw a crowd of lads where they were from, almost to the exact street, just by the tartan hanging off them.

At least, he thought that was how it started. Rod Stewart was getting going then too. They liked him as well, those teenage boys did: bluesy boozy Rod. One of the lads, wearing his Scottish heart with pride on his North London sleeve, thumping David Cassidy, so they said, for giving money to the IRA. Herbie had acquired a scarf himself – Royal Stewart tartan, funnily enough: blue, yellow, white, green and black on red – bought one day after school from a shop on Sandy Row that up till then only sold to old men and probably couldn't believe its luck. The shopkeeper asked him if he wanted it in a bag or was going to wear it home. 'Bag,' Herbie said, and as soon as he was out the door stuck that bag inside his school rucksack. He didn't take it out again until he was back home in his bedroom, door closed. And on him or off him, it never left that room again. He was too young for the gangs, and besides if his parents had seen him with it they'd have had his life: *That's not how we brought you up to be.*

Within a couple of years, tartan had been usurped by the Bay City Rollers and the teenage girls who worshipped them. In some places, the story was, the former Tartan gangs had been inducted wholesale into loyalist paramilitary groups. Round Herbie's way, it was more like ones and twos, if he could trust the evidence of his ears and eyes. The age of the people these boys, still in their teens, were suddenly associating with, the air they acquired of being beyond rebuke, beyond any common moral code. Some of them in the course of time became dumpers of bodies themselves, defilers.

Herbie tried to imagine back almost half a century. He tried to imagine the final moments of those three young soldiers, the grass verge, the night air, Belfast at its most beguiling below them, a magic carpet of lights.

Then bang, bang, bang: black.

He tried to imagine too the boy who had been him, angling the small mirror that sat on top of the chest of drawers so that he could admire himself in his jean jacket, the cuffs folded back on themselves, twice, to set off the scarf, cascading from the knot at his wrist over the back of his hand, bunching it in his fist, whirling it above his head as he had seen scores of other boys do, in sync, chanting. He had tried a few of the chants out too, under his breath. Words that even after fifty years brought the heat of shame to his cheeks.

No matter how hard he struggled to recognise him, it was important that he didn't lose sight of that boy and remembered to hold him to account.

Tanya suffered something of a setback the week after Beth was there. In the space of a couple of days she lost the rest of her hair and for a while looked as though the treatment was getting the better of her. Wretched was her word for it. Absolutely and completely wretched. When eventually she was too wretched even to talk, Martin took over the Skype duties. He and Herbie sitting at last face to face. The photos didn't really do him justice. He was, Herbie had to admit, easy on the eye.

'She's had a rough couple of days of it,' he said. 'You wouldn't wish it on your worst enemy. Tell you the truth, she sat and talked the other night about stopping the treatment altogether, but then…'

Actually, Herbie couldn't altogether follow what did come then, though it appeared to involve the sister-in-law of Martin's mother's cousin who had been through the wringer with this exact same thing and who had had the same thoughts as Tanya had, but was talked round eventually and never looked back, though it may have been any of the mother's cousin, the sister-in-law's partner or, potentially, the mother's cousin's partner (they were all name-checked), the talker-round, rather than the sister-in-law herself who was being offered in this instance as the god of special knowledge.

'I want you to know I'm taking care of her,' was where tale eventually led teller.

'I know you are,' Herbie said. 'And I really appreciate you letting me know, but I don't want you thinking I'm sitting here judging you…'

Martin cut across him. 'The love she had for you, that didn't disappear, it's in a different place now, but she knows where it is.'

'Toome.'

'What's that?'

'Sorry, I was… nothing.'

'I'm not doing this very well.'

'You are,' Herbie said.

'It's just other stuff, newer stuff, like me, has been added. She stopped loving you, but she didn't stop remembering that she loved you then. And, well, when I asked her to let me be with her, I was asking to be with all the things she was and had been, right back to the very start of her.' He smiled and shrugged in one. 'You're part of my life too, in a way.'

It was hard for him to say it, but Herbie knew Martin was part of his as well.

'Look after yourself,' came easier, so that's what he said and that's where they left it.

10

A Saturday morning. Just warm enough, with a jumper on, to sit out in the yard with the papers. All the home news stories were of things that should have been happening but weren't. He heard through the open back door the sound of the front gate being opened, the letterbox being pushed back then let go, the gate again, clacking on its latch.

A purple-liveried plane climbed at a forty-five-degree angle away from the airport to his right.

Beth came out and set the post on the bench beside him.

'Thank you,' he said.

She stood there, arms folded.

'Is there something you're not telling me?'

Probably a lot, but nothing he hadn't not been telling her for years already.

She pointed to the address stamped in the left corner of the top envelope. Doctor's surgery.

He had a moment of uncertainty himself as he worked his finger under the flap, with difficulty, and (difficulty doubled) took the letter out of the jagged opening he had made.

Writing this letter with considerable regret... wanted to take this opportunity to thank you for the privilege you afforded me of working with you and your family all these years...

'It's Dr Ross,' he told Beth, once his heart had stopped beating up into his throat, 'she's retiring.'

'Is that all?' She sounded almost disappointed. 'I thought she would have been gone long ago.' From inside the house now. 'She was old when I was a wee girl.' Head round the door frame again, pleased with herself. 'Old when God was.'

Herbie read on. Another doctor in the practice would be taking over her caseload. *Every confidence in his ability and expertise... no interruption to the excellent care that, I hope you will agree, you have always enjoyed and no need for you to do anything further...*

Actually – Herbie set the letter down – there was.

Plane coming in to land. Purple livery again. Looked like the same one coming back: *sorry, forgot something.*

A sudden gust of wind that might have been part of the same general disturbance lifted and separated the pages of the international news section and for a moment he was being offered – flash sale – a glimpse of how the world and all its parts fitted together if he could only blink and imprint it on his memory before...

The wind dropped. The paper settled again, messily.

First thing after Monday morning's school-run madness he took the two buses across town and got off in front of the row of shops – although only one of them was strictly speaking still a shop – round the corner from the health centre.

Dr Ross wasn't in, which he would have realised if he had had the foresight to make an actual appointment.

'Tell you the truth,' the receptionist said, 'she was more or less finished up before those letters even went out.'

'I want to change practice,' Herbie said.

'Right.' The receptionist was trying to fit a pile of pre-scriptions into an envelope, watched by a pony-tailed young man, who may or may not have been waiting to receive them. 'You know you didn't need to come here to do that? All you do is fill in a form at the place you want to transfer to and they take care of everything for you.'

'I did know.' He didn't. 'But I was nearby.'

'Of course. Still, I think it's better that you do it at the other end.'

The phone rang. 'Damn.' The receptionist put an elbow on the prescriptions and answered. 'Good morning, White Fields Practice.' The young man with the pony tail, realising there was just him and Herbie, took out his phone. 'Putting you through to the Treatment Room now,' the receptionist said. She looked at Herbie, clearly wondering why he was still there.

'Is there anything else I can help you with?'

'No, that was about it really.'

'In that case…'

'Yes.'

The receptionist went back to stuffing the prescriptions

GLENN PATTERSON

into the envelope. The young man put away his phone. Herbie made his way to the door.

What had he been expecting, after all, three cheers for Herbie? 'For He's a Jolly Good Fellow'?

He waited fifteen minutes for a bus back into town, during which time the only *shop* shop in the row facing him had exactly one customer. A goldmine, they used to call this part of the road.

A white-haired man across the aisle nodded as Herbie took his seat. The stop after, the same man leaned forward and called to another man who had just got on. 'Willie!'

Willie was in the process of lowering himself into one of the reduced mobility seats behind the driver's cab, but he hauled himself up by a chrome pole and staggered down the aisle, eyes narrowed, straining for focus.

'Who's that?' he said as he approached.

'What do you mean who's that? It's Kenny! Who's that!'

'Kenny! I haven't my glasses. Shift over.'

Kenny did, tight against the window. 'How you doing, apart from being blind?'

'The best.'

'Horses treating you well?'

'I'm a few shillings up.'

'You're in front then? Good for you. I've put six on since Saturday and not a winner among them. I think the last one's still running. Next time I hear of that one it'll be on Tesco's shelves.'

'Where you headed now?'

'Where do you think? Put another one on. Seventh time lucky, what?'

'Bookie's down the road from your house scud you?'

'Bookie's down the road from my house is no worse or no better than any other bookie's, but a change is as good as a rest, isn't that it? And sure I have my bus pass. Gets me out.'

'What age are you?'

'What age am I? A peeler wouldn't ask me that, or if he did I wouldn't tell him.'

'I'm sixty-seven next birthday.'

Kenny turned to face him. 'Sixty what? Sure you're only a wee lad.'

'I feel like one, I'll tell you that.'

'Something you're taking?'

'Better than that. I'm doing a line with a girl across the water… Here…' He had his phone out. It barely fitted in the palm of his hand. 'Look… No, wait, there she's there.'

'Flip me.' Kenny's admiration sounded completely genuine. 'I'd go across to see her myself. How'd you meet her?'

'Wrestling. I was over in Liverpool last month for the big title fight…'

'I didn't know you went in for that carry-on, but I'll let that pass.'

'And she was there with some girlfriends.'

'I'll let that pass too.'

'She told me she liked my shirt. Said how nice it was to meet a man who knew how to dress himself.'

'You've had the practice, did you tell her that?'

'I told her I didn't mind spending a bit of money, if that's what she meant.'

'You're right there. Those cheap ones, it's one wash then all they're good for is wiping floors.'

'Wiping your backside, more like.'

'Well, I didn't want to be ignorant with other people present.' Kenny took in Herbie and his fellow passengers with a sideways nod of the head.

'Matter of fact, that's what I'm heading into town for now,' Willie said, 'get a new one.'

'You going back over to see her?'

Willie was still looking at the phone. 'She's coming here. I'm just waiting on her calling with the date. She'd have been here before now only her landlord was acting the maggot, saying she owed him back rent. I sent her a few quid, get him off her back.'

Herbie saw Kenny give his friend a glance before turning his head and looking out the window. Wellington Place. City Centre. 'This is us,' Kenny said. He sounded relieved.

'Good luck with your horse.'

'Here's what I know about luck. D'you play cards? My da never went near a horse, but a great man for the cards. I saw him lose a hundred pound when a hundred pound was something, and people would be shaking their heads and saying, what do you think, Tommy, quit now? Live to fight another day? And here he'd be, fill my glass, deal me in, I'm not thinking of folding yet… Sooner or later, your fortune changes.'

'That's the spirit… I mind his funeral.'

'Ah, sure, it broke my mother's heart, the way he went.' Kenny shook Willie's hand at the bottom of the steps, held it tight a moment – 'Just you watch yourself, hear?' – then clapped him on the back. 'I'll see you again one of these years.'

'God willing: isn't that what they say?'

'Aye, when they don't know any better.'

Belfast was already at lunch. There were queues out all the doors. The Greggs the Costas the Starbucks the Nando's the sandwich bars noodle bars burrito bars the cafe bars the bar bars and newly sprouted patisseries. It was something to be seen. The sheer appetite. Herbie bought a bag of crisps to pass himself and sat on a bench in front of City Hall next to a couple feeding one another sushi with their fingers. Um, that one said, um-um, said the other. Um-um-um… Um-um-um-um. A woman walked up and down before them, smoking, talking on her phone and, by constant swapping of handset and cigarette, eating sweet potato fries from a cardboard pouch. On a balcony on the far side of the street a waiter offered a basket of bread rolls to a party of three who had been conversing in Sign. A toddler in a buggy being backed by his father out the Burger King doors pulled his gold card crown down over his eyes and ears and moved his head from side to side, revelling in the sudden nothing.

As he was standing up to put his crisp packet in the bin Herbie caught sight of Willie from the bus passing by with a Next bag and a Subway to-go box. He had packed a lot into his twenty minutes in town. Girl Across the Water could be calling at any moment. No time to hang around.

At the stop for Herbie's second bus, a young woman in a T-shirt that said 'Don't Even Think About It' placed a filled panini in front of a man sitting crosslegged on a blanket with his back to a telecoms box. The man at once tore off the top two inches and placed it under the muzzle of the whippet that until the panini hove into view had been dozing on the blanket beside him.

Um-um-um-um-*um*.

He was standing by the driver's cab of the bus, waiting for it to slow and set him down, when he saw Neeta come running out of the Post Office and cross the street, not even waiting for the lights to change, waving her apologies right-handed to the drivers coming this way, left-handed to the drivers coming that, the driver of Herbie's bus included. 'Yes, yes, yes… yes, yes, yes… I know, I know.'

'Did you ever see the like of that?' the driver said to Herbie, or to the world at large with Herbie just its nearest representative.

Herbie shook his head and then the second the bus doors were closed followed Neeta into Sam's.

She was still getting her breath back when he entered. Sam and Derek were both behind the counter. 'Are you ready for this?' Neeta asked and drew herself up to her full five foot two. 'I can tell you that your new neighbours-stroke-rivals over the way will be – drum roll, drum roll, splishy-splashy cymbals' – Derek took Sam's hand, squeezed – 'the Christians All Together Church.'

'The CATCH?' Derek uncoupled himself from Sam. 'In the name of fuck. If it's not a sin to say it now.'

'Not to them, it isn't,' Neeta said. 'Didn't you know? You can say it and do it as often as you like, drink too, I'm told. As long as you are sincerely questing after God the rest of the time. Maybe even at the same time.'

'For all have sinned and fallen short, or however it goes,' said Sam.

'So stop beating yourself up and have another Bloody Mary… in bed… with your next-door neighbour's husband, or wife, or both.'

'Is that going to be better or worse than Jamie Oliver, do you think?' Herbie asked.

'I'll say one thing for Jamie Oliver,' said Derek, 'you'd know where you stood with him. But that lot…? Have you seen them going in there on Sunday mornings? Look like they're coming home from Saturday night, half of them, and not a prayer group either. I liked it better when they wore shirts and ties and ridiculous hats. At least you could spot them and give them a wide berth.'

'I hear they're going to call it Clean,' Neeta said.

'Call what Clean?'

'Their restaurant.'

Sam shook his head. 'Of course they are.'

A silent moment or two ensued then Derek spoke again.

'You know if they're Clean what that makes us…'

Herbie told them about the incident with the wreath.

'Bit by bit,' said Sam, 'they are coming for us all.'

The Post Office was to close its doors for the last time at lunchtime on the final day of the tax year. After the prolonged lead-in the end was going to be swift.

'I knew it was coming, but all the same, I'm not sure, now I'm staring right down the barrel of it, how I'm going to cope,' Neeta said. She remembered when she was growing up, getting on a bus this one time with her mum and her wee sister and the driver refusing to take their fare. It was his sixty-fifth birthday: retirement day. He had this journey and then he was taking the bus back to the depot, and that was him, finished. He was letting everyone he picked up on free. Here he was to them, 'What are they going to do to me? Give me the sack?'

(The Happy Bus, her wee sister had called it for years after. 'When are we getting the Happy Bus again?')

Neeta wished she could do something to equal it – international postage for the price of a domestic second-class stamp, £10 on every senior citizen's electricity top-up card.

The thought sometimes was enough, Herbie told her.

'Here's another thought,' she said. 'I could slip a pound coin into one of those Monday morning bags of cash, you know, take it over the legal limit for deposits…' She savoured it a long moment then caught herself on. 'Ah, all right, I'll just give out free bags of Haribo to any kids that come in.'

'I'm not slagging off your customers, but I don't think you'll be down many bags of Haribo by the end of the day.'

A couple of days later the CATCH called in person. Persons. Herbie had the whole thing from Derek.

A delegation of four – 'cell' was their own preferred term (theirs and the Provisional IRA's) – who were – their term again – *reaching out* to neighbours on this part of the road, hoping to scotch rumours and allay fears. 'We're just ordinary folks, who happen to love the Lord,' their spokesperson/OC said, 'as crazy and mixed up as any other group of eleven and a half thousand people...' She let that number sit a moment... 'well, last time we were able to count.'

She indicated one of the cell's number – Kim – adding pointedly that they (singular) were from the LGBTQIA+ group. 'I think you would be surprised,' Kim said, 'the way attitudes have changed. Churches like ours are probably the most forward-thinking and accepting parts of this entire society.'

Sam was studying a leaflet another of the cell had handed him. 'What's this about Clean Thursdays?'

'Oh, yeah,' said the OC, 'they are like a healthy alternative to Bring Your Own. We're going to have nutritionists and mindfulness therapists on hand, six o'clock to nine o'clock. You should give them a go.'

'We're sort of busy ourselves on Thursday nights.'

'Well, if that changes any time, you won't have far to come to find us.'

On the way out the door, they gave the Radio Ga Ga salute.

Sam didn't even wait for the door to shut but flew around the restaurant, gathering up Scrabble tiles from this table and that, and that, and that, and that: the D, the I, the C, the K, the S. He placed them in a line facing out across the street.

'I don't care how comfortable they are with the word, I don't care how comfortable they are with what any of us do with ours,' he said. 'I don't want anyone to move those letters. Ever.'

11

Tanya had another appointment with the specialist in Cork City. Beth would hear nothing but that she would go with her. 'It's not that I don't trust Martin,' she said to Herbie. 'It's just that I don't trust Martin.'

'And Micky and Roza?'

'They'll get somebody in. It's only a couple of days.'

'Did you ever talk to Paul again?'

'Every other day. He's all caught up with this new thing.'

'Not more driving?'

'No, this is more of a solo venture.'

'"I would tell you, but then I would have to kill you."'

She laughed. 'Not quite.'

Herbie nodded. 'I thought I saw him the other day coming out of the Post Office, but by the time I got off the bus he was gone. Good he's got something, whatever it is.'

Beth phoned, as before, late on the night of the day that she left for Schull. 'It's unbelievable,' she said, 'the change in her. Talk about darkest hour just before dawn.' The specialist at the conclusion of another Ultra HD tour of Tanya's insides concurred. Whistled his admiration in fact.

'I'm inclined to tell you not to come back and see me for another six months,' he said.

'Of course,' Tanya said, 'that might just mean he is jetting off somewhere between now and then.'

'Choppering.'

Beth hadn't said when exactly she would be back. Evening, Herbie presumed, of whichever day. So he was surprised, coming home a couple of afternoons later, to find her sitting on the sofa surrounded by the boxes of photographs from the spare-now-her room, looking as though she had been going through them for an hour or two already. Martin had some business up in Dublin, leaving Schull first thing. She was able to hitch a ride with him right into Connolly Station. 'Like, right inside,' she said. 'One of his uncles used to work on the cross-border mail deliveries – showed him how to come round the back and up beside the platform for the Belfast train. I hadn't the heart to tell him I was booked on the bus, and there was a train sitting there waiting to board…'

Herbie had cleared a space on the sofa and sat down beside her.

'You don't mind me lifting these all down?'

'Why would I mind? They're as much yours as mine.'

'I don't remember ever seeing the half of them,' she said. 'Look at you in this. Where was that?'

He took the photo out of her hand. His eyes slid off the not much more than boy who had been him to the cathedral door before which he stood, the bronze rail to the left of it, endlessly repeating the same sight gag, and the legend accompanying it, *à mon seul desir*.

'Saarbrücken, Germany.'

'You must be... what, sixteen, seventeen?'

'Eighteen just turned.'

'Is that not about the time you met Mum?'

'Same week, practically.'

'Really? In Germany?'

'We must have told you the story,' he started to say, but – 'Oh, my God, why did you ever let me out of the house in this?' – she had already moved on. 'Little Lady Gagaaaah.' She mimed fingers down her throat. With good reason. Flowers and stripes. And frills. And knee-length lace-up basketball boots. In blue camouflage. What could he and Tanya have been thinking?

'You were very strong-willed, or we were very weak.'

'And *this* one...'

Velvet headband and bow on bald baby head.

'Ah, now that one was your granny's doing. She had bought you it and we didn't want to hurt her feelings. You never had it on you again after we took the photo. She had it framed.'

They sat together until the light went, swapping pictures, trying to put names to faces – she could still manage an impressive twenty-three out of twenty-seven of her Primary One class photo – supplementing or subtly correcting one another's memories.

He told her about the feeling he got now and then that he

had somehow been separated from his own past, or pasts, 'like someone else has been using my identity.'

'Or you've *taken on* someone else's, did you ever think about that? That your life is actually just a script you have learned by heart or a chip that's been inserted.'

A little later: 'It crossed my mind, you know, when the whole bankruptcy thing was starting to happen... Press delete and upload a whole other me... or other her, I suppose it would be. I actually had a number some woman I knew gave me. I carried it around in my purse for weeks.'

'What do you mean, a number? Are you telling me you would have just disappeared on us?'

'Oh, I kept thinking about how I would find a way to let you know, even though this woman had said to me, only use that number if you're really, really serious about this.'

'That's a bit – what do you call the series that was on, the chemistry teacher in Arizona?'

'*Breaking Bad*? That's New Mexico, but, yeah, her whole world, I think, was a bit *Breaking Bad*.'

'Nice people you've been hanging out with.'

'I met her in court, as a matter of fact, well, in the cafeteria, between hearings...'

'I thought you told me you did it online?'

'I said you *could* do it. There were other people involved. I'd really rather not talk about it.'

'I'm sorry,' he said. 'You were in the cafeteria.'

'I was.' She seemed to be in two minds whether or not to go back there to finish the story. She came in, as it were, through another door. 'Have you ever been in the cafeteria of a court? My advice? Don't. It'll crush whatever fight you might have had in you just looking around you in there, although even without that it was a pretty persuasive pitch your woman gave me. Said I'd be surprised the people I talked to every day who weren't who everyone else took them to be.'

'What stopped you in the end?'

'Honestly? Money. If I'd had enough to pay to do that I would never have got into all that debt to begin with.' Her voice trailed off. 'Sorry, I should have said to you or Mum I was feeling that way, but I was all the time writing notes to you in my head, leaving clues. I suppose that means I was never ever likely to go through with it.'

The conversation was getting uncomfortably close in its terms to suicide, which he guessed her desire to disappear like that was a form of. He picked out a photo at random from a Boots envelope that had long ago lost its flap. 'Recognise that one?'

She leaned in, looking, pushing her hair behind her ears. 'Edinburgh. What am I, seven? The bake on me!'

Her grin was principally gum.

'We were only there five nights and you lost three front teeth. It was like every time you had something more solid than soup set before you' – he made a cluck sound – 'there'd go another one. People in the hotel were giving you money, in case the tooth fairy couldn't find you. You came back with more than you took away.'

'You know what I remember about that holiday? You and Mum kissing.'

'Oh, come on, we kissed a lot.'

'That wasn't the way it seemed to me.'

'Maybe we were just waiting all the other times until we knew you weren't looking.'

'I have a memory, up at the castle, whatever overtook the pair of you, you were like mwah-mwah-mwah.'

He didn't know how to tell her, but he was as certain as he could be about anything that the three of them never made it to the castle together on that trip. Tanya had come down with something or, no: done something – that's right, she had turned her ankle the night before. He had to go out and find a Boots to buy an elasticated bandage. Had he picked up a magazine as well? He could nearly see himself in the newsagent's on the Royal Mile.

Company, she used to read.

'You stay here and rest that, I'll take Beth.'

'If you're sure.'

'Sure I'm sure.'

Or something like that. Maybe Beth wasn't wrong though about the kissing. There was something, now that he thought about it, later that very day possibly, the wildness that came of trying not to make any noise. He could imagine next day they would have still been desperate to cling on to some of that, taking every opportunity to touch, handholding, neck-stroking, kissing.

He stood. 'Do you want tea?' he said.

'Mm.'

As he was opening the cupboard for the teabags he caught sight of her briefly, reflected in the door's high-shine surface, raised up slightly on one hip. Was she…? She was: slipping the photo into her pocket. He let the door close gently. He didn't know whether he had a negative, but no matter. She needed it more than he did.

He opened the fridge, took the milk out and sniffed – OK, probably, just. He had a look while he was at it to see if they had the wherewithal for dinner. Again, probably, just. He brought the mugs through, holding out the one in his left hand.

'That's yours there with just a splash…' He stopped. Beth had pulled over another box and was sitting flipping the pages of a small red notebook.

She frowned. 'What's all this?'

'Ah, now, now, careful with that. That's research stuff I've to sort through.'

'It looks like just a lot of names.'

'Yes, well, that's genealogy for you.'

'No, I mean the same names over and over and over…' She ran her finger along a line. 'One, two, three, four – five of them.'

He set the mugs down on the floor and went to take the notebook from her hand, but she dropped it on the sofa and reached into the box for another. She flicked through a couple of pages.

'This one's the same,' she said. She reached again for another. 'And this one.'

He picked up the first one she had cast aside, read the first page, the second, the third, jumping then to the last.

'Ah, Sean,' he said.

He didn't recognise a single one of the five, but he knew without having to check they were the names of the people who had been murdered in Sean's bar.

He sat on the sofa again next to his daughter, who looked into his eyes, trying to read them.

'Not what you were expecting?' she said.

He was about to say no, not at all, but stopped himself, or himself stopped him. This was a man whose life had been saved by a Toffo that he didn't even remember he had in his pocket, that he might on another day just have tossed in the bin. (Was any sweet worth the effort of all that sticky paper?) Bullets that might otherwise have struck him, ending their journey right there or continuing, on the far side of him, at a different trajectory, carried on uninterrupted into five other human beings of his acquaintance.

That's how he got to stand greeting newcomers in the entrance of the Records Office reading room and to go home every evening to his wife and his dinner and his shed.

Really, what else did Herbie expect?

He put all the notebooks back in their box, folded the lid over.

'I'm sorry,' Beth said.

'It's not your fault. Really.'

★

He opened his eyes. Voices coming out of the walls.

No. Not possible.

He hadn't opened his eyes. He had only dreamed that he had. The voices weren't real. They would go away.

They didn't, they must be, and he wasn't able to dream his eyes closed again: he was awake.

He reached for his phone, pressed the home button: 02.03. He had hardly been asleep at all. He realised, in the space of that movement, over the edge of the bed for the phone and back, that it was only one voice he had been hearing – Beth's, of course – but that it was coming from more than one spot. She must be walking up and down in there.

He strained, listening, but her voice was pitched too low, conscious of him perhaps, on the other side of the wall, not sleeping, straining, listening.

He tried to cover his ears with his pillow. *This is not your concern. This is not your concern.*

She was already downstairs making breakfast when he got up in the morning. She still had no idea how to slice bread. There was more on the floor than on the board. 'I've been thinking,' she said. She pressed the lever of the toaster. 'It's probably time I went back.'

'Oh.'

'I thought you'd be glad to get me out from under your feet.'

'You're not under my feet.' Though the heel of the bread she had butchered was.

'Glad that I was getting my act together at least.'

'I am, of course, I just wasn't expecting, you know, until your year was… I mean leases and things like that, are you even going to be able to find a place to live?'

'My friend Abbie has a room.' Maybe that was who she was talking to last night. Maybe 2 a.m. wasn't late at night in Abbie's life. 'She says I'd be doing her a favour taking it, somebody in the flat when she's away. Also, she has a bath, one of those big old-fashioned enamel ones with the brass taps, so you know…'

It might have been hurtful if it had sounded for a moment as though she actually meant it.

'When do you think you might go?'

'I don't know, Tuesday morning maybe?'

This was Thursday.

'Wow, that really is…'

'Soon, I know, but it just sort of came up.'

'But what about work?'

'Tell you the truth, I think they have been waiting for an opportunity to let me go. They've got a cousin, just lost his job with a precast concrete firm down in Tyrone, he's having a complete career rethink.'

For some reason his father came into his mind, chasing a start halfway across the city the day he was handed his cards from the shipyard. Maybe he would have fared better in today's world of work than Herbie himself had. Maybe Herbie's own generation, in time, would come to look like the anomaly, brought up to expect security, unable to adapt quickly enough to setbacks and reversals. Which only made him wish the harder for a future free from either for his daughter and all the generations coming behind her.

Her toast popped, charred at the thinnest corner. 'It's been good for me, this, being here. I don't want to be too melodramatic…'

'That wouldn't be like you.'

You're so funny, her face said, till her mouth overrode, 'It probably saved me.'

'Well, that really fills me with confidence for your going.'

'Listen, I'm ready for anything. I'll be fine.'

It was on the tip of his tongue to ask her if she couldn't set her sights a little higher, but talk about do as I say not as I do…?

He held his tongue while he got his own breakfast. Joined her at the table. That was long enough. He needed to talk to blank out the thought of the house without her.

'We should do something, go out.'

She turned her phone face down by her plate. 'Are they still doing BYO Thursdays round the corner?'

'Somewhere else, I meant. There's a whole clatter of places in town I've never even set foot in.'

'I'm sure that would be lovely. I was just thinking, but, it would be nice to see everyone before I went, say goodbye.'

He wasn't sure that wouldn't just make matters worse for him, but, 'All right,' he said, 'round the corner it is then.'

As he was getting up from the table with the dishes she was turning her phone face up again.

He looked back from the doorway.

'You would tell me if there was something wrong, wouldn't you?'

'I would, but there isn't.'

Business at Sam's had not yet recovered fully from the unfortunate incident of the rat in the yard, and this close to closing the Post Office crowd understandably had other things on their mind. Even at half past seven the cafe had an after-hours feel, couples and fews in deep conversation around candles craggy with wax. The craggiest stood atop the piano at which Kurtis Bain sat, sporting a moustache several shades darker than his dirty fair hair. (Beth said she was pretty sure she knew the exact Boots mascara he had used to enhance it: Natural Collection Definition Brown Black.) The suit had given way to a collarless striped shirt and braces, one strap of which was short of a button at the front to cling to. He sang tonight as though he had experienced deep and recent heartache. Goodbye George and Ira, hello Bessie Smith.

'Girlfriend transferred to a college across the water,' Derek explained to Herbie and Beth. 'Told him the night before she went, she thought it was better if they Took a Break. From one another, that is. Word has reached him that she is energetically pursuing other options.'

'I didn't even know they were college age,' Herbie said.

'She is, he isn't. Doesn't do his GCSEs until this May.'

'Rough.'

'You're telling me.' He looked about the room, no more than one table in three taken. 'I'm beginning to think he's more of a turn-off than the rat.'

'You want to tell him there are plenty more fish in the sea, don't you?'

Derek shook his head. 'He knows there aren't, not for him. There was only her and she's wriggled off the hook.'

'See, just there is where the metaphor becomes really icky,' Beth said.

Emmet and Yolanda had kept them a seat (not that there was competition) at the same table they were at last time they were all four there. 'We never miss,' Emmet said.

'I tell him, at least it's one night in the week he doesn't have to cook,' said Yolanda. 'Beth thinks I'm joking.' (Beth was not left the room to say she thought no such thing.) 'It's nothing to do with this...' She patted the arm of the folded wheelchair (Beth mutely signalled she had not presumed that it was). 'I just never cared much for it.'

'She made dinner for us a couple of times when we were first together,' Emmet chipped in. 'My stomach didn't care much for it either.'

'Remember the steak sausage, beetroot and black bean stir fry?'

Emmet covered his face with his hands, stifling a sob, much to Yolanda's evident delight.

'I was doing fusion cooking before anyone here had even heard of it.'

'Yeah, nuclear.'

Kurtis Bain was mumbling through 'Old Boyfriends' – 'Remember when you were burning for them, why do you keep turning them into Old Boyfriends' – as Derek and Sam served the main courses, as always on a Thursday a straight choice between one thing and another. (Beth ordered one thing, Herbie the other.) Tom Waits, if he'd heard the kid, would have tipped his hat in admiration, and maybe sidled up to him afterwards and suggested he get out now and again and skateboard with his friends.

They ate a while in companionable silence. Beth set down her knife and fork.

'I'm going to miss this,' she said. 'In fact – and, forgive me, this is not a sentence I would have imagined saying nine months ago – I'm going to miss Belfast.'

'It has a way of sneaking up on you, all right,' Emmet said.

'Some bits of it, mind you... maybe not so much.'

'Everywhere has its downside.'

'Yeah, but not everywhere makes it a part of their tourist industry. I keep thinking, they should stop their tour buses outside that pizza place where Paul was working and explain to people, those ridiculous-looking masked gunmen in all those murals you've been photographing...? This is mostly what they were getting up to, when they weren't playing around in the big scary dressing-up box, what they are still getting up to, extorting money and pushing people around.'

'Have you seen any of the new murals?' Yolanda, this. 'I said it a while ago to Emmet: look, the masks have started to come off! They're all walking around in their civvies and smiling, like, what were you so afraid of, it was only us?'

'Oh, good, maybe next we'll actually see them standing over some poor guy kneeling in a ditch with his mouth taped up, or walking away from a kid they're just after shooting in the knees.'

'Or a big order of unpaid-for pizzas.'

Yolanda proposed a toast to Paul: may whatever he does next *be allowed to* turn out right.

Late in the second set (the take-it-or-leave-it this evening was treacle pudding: all present took) Herbie passed a note up to Kurtis Bain telling him Beth was leaving town and asking him to play something for her. 'Whatever you think,' he wrote, realising that that, in the pianist's present mood, might just be asking for it.

Kurtis Bain stroked his moustache a long moment (kudos to Boots Natural Collection Definition Brown Black, it didn't streak or smudge) then set the note on top of the piano, nodded over: *I've got this.* 'For Beth,' was all he said, an octave lower than Kurtis Mark 1, as his fingers began to glide across the keyboard, brushing keys, looking for purchase on the tune. It took Herbie a good twenty seconds to work out what it was, the angle that the kid came at it, the fact that it was several decades outside of his normal repertoire, but at last it settled – he settled – into 'Changes'. The conversations that had been carrying under and occasionally above the last few songs (it had actually seemed a politeness not to eavesdrop on the wee lad's grief) stopped as the other diners recognised it too and turned themselves to face him, strangely fascinated.

His improvising stretched it into a fifth and then a sixth minute and still no one spoke or stirred. (Sam and Derek, framed in the doorway, slipped an arm around one another's waist.) Pretty soon now every single one of them was going to get older. Pretty soon now this moment too and all that so vividly led up to it would be the distant past, a flat line in history, irretrievable beneath the layers of Belfasts, worlds, yet to come, all their coffee rituals, their wheelie bins, their BYO music nights, as arcane as tithes.

In the Kurtis Bain biopic (Herbie couldn't be sure Kurtis Bain himself wasn't already at work on it, starring in it, even) that could well turn out to be the moment when things took an upward turn for him: the applause, the tears fought back. He leaned his head forward until it was almost resting on the piano, whistling the final saxophone solo, which he brought to a close with a whisper of a chord.

'Is it sacrilege to say I never liked that song?' Beth said under her breath. 'Up to now, I mean.'

'A guy I used to go out with gave me a copy of the lyrics for my fourteenth birthday,' said Yolanda. 'Like, I'd asked him for them, but you know, I was imagining handwritten parchment or something – he was actually a lovely writer – a nice frame. He'd just torn it out of a magazine, *Disco 45*, wasn't that what you called it? Hadn't even trimmed the margin. I ch-ch-ch-chased the skitter out of the house. It was two years before I got another snog off anyone.'

'That'll teach you,' said Emmet.

'Good job it didn't. I had another half dozen to send packing before I got to you.'

As people were beginning to reach for their coats at the evening's end, Sam brought Beth out a hastily iced Good Luck muffin. 'It's date and walnut... just in case you have any allergies.'

'Only to making speeches.'

'You are absolved. Anyway, we expect to see you back here next Christmas.'

'At the latest,' Derek said.

She went across and had a word with Kurtis Bain, who listened then put his arms around her and smiled: actually smiled.

'Can I ask you what you said?' Herbie asked her.

'No, but it didn't involve fish.'

Kurtis Bain cracked his fingers a couple of times and placed them back on the keys, trying something else out. Herbie had no idea what, but he took the line, if that was what it was he was singing, out on to the street with him.

The road was absolutely still in both directions, not so much as a distant taillight. The city had a way of doing that, even now, emptying out. It suggested that there was still spare capacity somewhere. It was just a question of sitting down and figuring it out to everyone's advantage. He hummed that last line of Kurtis Bain's, hearing the words in his head. The moment you know you know you know.

'Where Are We Now?' Beth said. 'That that you're humming.'

And she joined in.

12

He barely saw her at all Friday, and Saturday morning again she was gone almost as soon as she was up. A few last bits and pieces to sort out at work, she said. Or he thought she said.

Late on Saturday afternoon – he was just coming back from a match: another 0–0 – Roza and Micky called at the door.

By their van, parked out front, did he know them. If he had had to pick them out in a line-up otherwise, he would have passed them over as out of scale with the stories told about them. Micky couldn't have been more than five foot three, Roza only a hairsbreadth taller.

'I thought Beth was at the office,' Herbie said.

'Oh, she might have gone in,' Roza said. 'We were out on the road all day.'

'Not much of it actual road,' said Micky. He handed Herbie a box. 'We just wanted to leave this off in person. It's a wee bit fragile. Black crystal.'

'Black Tyrone crystal,' said Roza. 'Last of its kind.'

He invited them in, but they said no, thank you, they had

better get going if they wanted to have a full Saturday night at home, although... Roza had turned as though to leave and then turned back, 'I couldn't ask you for a glass of water, could I?'

So, in they both stepped, and in the time that it took Herbie to let the water run cold enough to drink did a complete recce of the entire downstairs, little glances passing – instinctively, it looked – between them. (Two sets of eyebrows rising in appreciation of the neat little yard.) You never knew when you would need a particular kind of place.

Beth was coming in the front gate as Herbie was opening the door to let them out.

If she was surprised – or in any way caught out – to see them she didn't show it.

'I saw the van,' she said. Which might have accounted for the lack of surprise. She opened her bag. 'Your keys.'

'You could just have left them with the doorman.'

'I know, but you like to make absolutely sure, don't you?'

Roza put her arms around her. '*Feliĉo en ĉio, kio postulas,*' she said.

'Happiness in all that comes after,' Micky said, by way of translation and reinforcement, and wriggled his way into the clinch with them.

'I don't think they had been expecting you to go into work today,' Herbie said when they had gone.

'No?'

'You did go in, didn't you?'

'I stopped by... Wait' – she looked at him, incredulous

WHERE ARE WE NOW?

– 'are you checking up on me? What do you think I was up to?'

Which was a good question, and one to which he had absolutely no answer.

He shook his head, 'Falling into old habits... Me, not you.'

She had opened the gift box and lifted out one of the glasses, from which she removed the tissue paper. 'They are beautiful.'

'Roza says last of its kind.'

She looked at him.

'Factory's gone. The whole industry. About five years ago.'

She wrapped the tissue paper round the glass and – gently, gently – set it back in the box again. 'Would you be OK if I left these here? Just for the time being. I mean they literally are irreplaceable now.'

While they were having dinner on her last night (of course he cooked leeks, in a pie, with mustard and nutmeg), she told him that he wasn't to bother himself coming to the airport with her in the morning. 'I'll just be straight out of the taxi and in through security.'

'This is George Best City Airport you're talking about,' he said. 'The closest the taxi can drop you is a hundred yards away.'

In an age where air travel had been recast into a set of ever stiffer challenges for travellers to overcome, Belfast's airport had excelled itself by making the first and last steps – dropping off and picking up – as awkward and frustrating as anything that lay in between.

'That means it will be even more of a dash,' Beth said. 'Anyway, I don't want to be making it into a whole big goodbye. I'd much rather just go out the way I came in, me and a taxi driver, you at the front gate.'

He decided not to press her on it, but when he looked at her again across the table next morning as she sat at breakfast, an expression on her face that called to mind the day she started secondary school, cheerfulness stretched so tight it only accentuated the apprehension underlying, he had a second change of heart.

'It's big for me, you know, you leaving, no matter how soon I'm going to see you again. I want to say goodbye properly.'

She looked down at her hands beneath the table.

'We've time yet,' he said.

'What?'

'I thought you were checking your clock.'

'Yes. Sorry. You're right, we've time.'

'Would you rather I booked the taxi now anyway?'

'Is that bad of me?'

'Not at all.'

'Then, maybe, yes, just to be safe.'

She went upstairs to finish packing. Less than ten minutes it took. The rucksack, slumped in the hallway, looked as full, or as empty, as when she first arrived, which is to say about half.

The taxi driver asked her, as she took it and put it in the boot, if Beth was heading across the water to a festival.

Beth said she thought her festival days were maybe behind her.

'You're as well out of here, then,' the driver said. The T-shirt under her leather jacket proclaimed there was no such thing as luck. 'It's flipping festivals from one end of the year to another now. If they found a day where there wasn't a festival happening, they would probably have a festival to celebrate it.'

She asked Herbie when they arrived at the airport if she wanted him to keep the meter running: easier than having to book another taxi.

'It's OK,' he said, 'I'll maybe just get a bus into town.'

'Just as long as you don't get into one of these airport cabs,' the driver said. 'Sit here waiting on work walking up to them while the rest of us are out chasing our tails all day, then charge you extra for the privilege.'

There was some confusion at the bag drop counter when the airline rep asked Beth if Herbie was her travelling companion.

She leaned in across the counter. 'I'm travelling alone,' she said, and the rep looked at the screen and said, 'Oh. Right.' And typed some more.

He walked back through the concourse with her as far as the covered corridor leading down to security. Passengers only beyond this point. Last chance to stock up on Tayto Crisps! The Taste of Home!

He thought he detected a last-minute hesitation. 'You're absolutely sure you're going to be all right?'

'I am, a hundred per cent.'

'All right, but no more talking to strange women in courthouse cafeterias?'

'No more of that, promise.' She squeezed his hand.

He tried to slip his other hand into her pocket. She trapped it with her elbow, it and the £200 in twenties he had meant to leave in there.

'Oh, no you don't,' she said.

'Just to tide you over the first few days. Look,' pre-empting her next objection, 'they're Bank of England and everything.'

She shook her head, you seriously don't need to do this, but she must have realised there was no winning this one.

To their right, the terminal doors parted and the space was filled by a large party in navy-and-white tracksuits – school team, it looked like, for a sport designed specifically to use up as much as possible of their excess energy and requiring a whole clatter of bags and equipment tipping off the trolleys that clashed repeatedly as they pushed them to where a coach or teacher (smaller than the smallest of them by several inches) took up position and tried to call them all to order.

'I wouldn't want to be stuck behind them in security,' Herbie said, while they were both still looking.

'No.' Beth's eyes flicked up towards the clock bracketed to the ceiling. 'I guess I'd better go on through.'

She stretched up to kiss his cheek and in the next instant

was round the corner, down the corridor, and that was her, gone.

He stood a while looking at the place where she wasn't, not entirely sure what his next step should be.

The school team coach was moving among his charges, collecting passports.

'Just one each,' he was saying. 'I don't care if you have two, I just want one from each of you.'

And suddenly, Herbie knew exactly what his next step would be: next two or three thousand.

Long ago, when George Best Belfast City was still the Harbour Airport, and a quarter of a mile nearer the city centre, you had been able to walk out of the compound (was what it was in those Troubled days) and straight up a footbridge over the dual carriageway to a railway halt, from where, if you were fortunate enough to arrive at one of those twice-hourly moments (once hourly on Sundays) when trains actually did halt, you could be in the city centre in minutes. If instead of taking the footbridge you had turned right, you would have arrived, by way of the apparent sight gag that was the East Belfast Yacht Club, at Victoria Park, then a somewhat isolated and dingy place of public resort, now the beneficiary of much council love and investment, with landscaped paths connecting to the greenway that in turn connected to the road leading up to Herbie's house and, before that, the Post Office.

It was the last week of trading. He could pick up his Irish passport form and say his goodbyes at the same time. Two birds, one stone.

He was pleased to discover, turning out the main gate, that the footpath had followed the airport all the way to its new location. Almost as soon as he set foot on it, though, he understood why he might have doubted it – why he had never, in the more than fifteen years since the airport's eastward translation, seen a single person walk along it. The traffic hurtling by was truly terrifying, tugging at his sleeve, his trouser leg, wanting to suck him into its slipstream (and, yes, it was in his mind the whole time, Beth's friend and all that flowed from his error of judgement coinciding with the relentless march to digital-only broadcasting). He was never in his life so glad, reaching the little side gate into the park, to step in goose shit. The geese responsible – year-round residents, these, who had long since adopted Belfast ways – sized him up for edibles then, nah, turned their backs and looked for the next likely human.

He had gone about twenty yards when he saw a young seagull, its brown feathers just beginning to turn white, standing right in his path. He tilted his head to the left, looking at it. It tilted its head to the right, looking back at him. It couldn't be. Could it? He didn't suppose it was all that far from its normal flapping ground, and that spot on its bill just beginning to turn red looked more than generically familiar. He clucked at it, encouragingly, rubbing the pads of his forefinger and thumb together, all the while trying with his other hand to slide his phone out of his pocket to take a picture, but as soon as the seagull saw the object in his hand it spread its wings and rushed at him, beak open.

He only just managed to pull his hand out of the way in time. The seagull lifted off the ground and landed a few feet away. It looked over its shoulder at him – a look that said, remember, I only need to be lucky once – then went about its grooming.

The Post Office was jammed to overflowing.

Should have guessed.

It looked, as he drew near, as though half of east Belfast had just remembered it was the last week too. The senior, non-Haribo-eating half, in the main. Some fella was actually part walking, part riding his scooter up and down the footpath, looking for a way through the press of bodies out front and on to the road. He had a helmet on that wouldn't have looked out of place on a bike ten times as powerful and he seemed to jerk his head in Herbie's direction not once but twice, as he finally got clear before put-put-putting through the gaps in the road traffic and off down a side street, though he may simply have been checking over his shoulder, making sure there was nothing coming behind him, or no one.

Herbie went into Sam's: give it twenty minutes, see if the crowd across the road thinned. A few of those minutes passed. A few minutes in which Herbie chatted to Derek – yes, Beth had got away, or got as far as the airport anyway, early, which was unlike her – ordered his coffee and took it to his favourite table beneath the capital S. Observed his customary prayerful pause. O, Avatar of Simple Pleasures.

There was a sound then – *kkkrrrkkkhh* – like a rip in the everyday.

Herbie looked up. A big black BMW had slewed in at an angle right in front of the Post Office (the rip was its handbrake being yanked), paying no heed to the giant *BUS STOP* painted, in yellow, on the road beneath its axle. No heed paid either to the traffic that began almost at once building up behind by the two occupants who got out, leaving their doors wide open, and went into the Post Office then came back out half a minute later, two become four, looking this way and that for a person, a thing even, on which to vent their collective rage. Variously they pulled down the drawer of a metal bin, stuck an arm in a post box, shook their fists in faces of passersby. One of them strode out into the road as though intent on Sam's – everyone in there had by now congregated at the window around Herbie's table – just as a double-decker bus came along, city-bound. The bus driver jammed his foot on the brake, his fist on the horn. The fella in the road didn't even flinch. He slapped the bus's windscreen – Herbie would have sworn it shook – and when the bus driver still didn't let up with the horn went round and tried to pull the folding doors open with his bare hands. Other drivers on the blind side of the bus started tooting their horns too. The fella let go the bus doors and went and smacked a couple of car roofs – *Fuck do you want?* (Nothing, their drivers' faces said, they wanted nothing ever again, ever, ever, ever) – then he and his mates got back into their own car, reversed, went forward, reversed in a looping arc and drove off up the road, one door still flapping.

Derek broke the silence that had fallen in the cafe. 'I wouldn't want to be sitting at home waiting on him coming back tonight.'

The police arrived half a minute later, putting on their caps as they got out of their car, adjusting them, using up another few seconds before going into the Post Office. 'What's the betting,' said Sam, 'they were sitting round the corner, waiting till they heard that BMW go?'

'Well, you wouldn't want to create a whole scene,' Derek said. 'You wouldn't want to run the risk you'd actually have to lift those fellas.'

While all of this was going on, Herbie's phone rang. Unknown caller. He nearly wasn't going to answer. *No, I didn't have a recent accident at work. Yes, I think I would remember...*

But then he thought it might be Beth, using a call box to save her battery. He pressed the little green phone symbol.

'Herbie?'

'Who's this?'

'It's me: Paul. I've done something really stupid.' What he sounded was really excited. 'I lifted one of their bags.'

'Whose?'

'Theirs.'

Herbie heard again the sound of that handbrake. He saw the bus windscreen shake with the force of a slap. He remembered the guy in the motorcycle helmet, as he was arriving, jerking his head at him: definitely, he thought now, he was jerking it at him.

'Wait, was that you on the scooter?'

'You were looking straight at me. I thought you must have known.'

To Herbie's shame his first thought was for his own phone, the trace… Could *they* do that? He got up and walked down the cafe and out the back to the yard.

'Where are you?'

There was heavy traffic noise in the background.

'Well away,' Paul said, 'and staying.'

'Is it worth all this for nine thousand pounds?'

'It's not the nine thousand, though don't worry, that'll not go to waste. It's beating them, just once.'

Herbie looked back into the body of the cafe. Beyond the heads at the window he could see the commotion continuing on the street.

'And in case you're worried,' Paul said, 'I bought this phone this morning and I'm standing with it right next to a bin.'

'I wasn't thinking of that,' he lied, but before he was even halfway through he was talking to himself.

It was only later – taking his seat again in the window – that he wondered how Paul had managed to get his number on a phone he had never used before. And in the next instant it occurred to him that the noise he was hearing while they were on the phone might not have been cars, but planes.

He tried Beth but she wasn't picking up. He started composing a text. Then stopped. Started again. Stopped again. He couldn't for the life of him think what it was he wanted to say. Or ask.

The whole episode was like... like something out of one of those old black-and-white comedies. That was Neeta's verdict, once the police had gone and she was able finally to slip across the road. You know, Alec Guinness and Alastair Sim and what do you call him, did *Jackanory* – Cribbins. The guy comes up to the counter, same as he does every week, lifts his carrier bag, pulls it open and... His eyes are practically out on stalks. *What the fuck*, he says.

(Bit strong for a black-and-white comedy that, they all agreed.)

He starts chucking about these bundles of printer paper, it looks like, cut roughly to banknote size and held together with elastic bands. He turns to his mate standing at the next window. 'Is this some sort of fucking joke?' His mate opens his bag wide for all that little world to see. No – *money, money, money, money* – his is all right. They stare at each other. They turn around, look at everyone in the queue, looking back open-mouthed at them. Push them, knock one old woman's shopping all over the floor. (Four tins of carrots. That's all.) 'What did you fucking do with it? What did you fucking do with it?'

It was when they threatened to block the door that Neeta slipped into the back and called the police, though by then one of them had already been on his phone reporting to his hoody friends, who turned up like the BMW cavalry and went through the whole what-did-you-fucking-do-with-it routine again, only louder. Practically screaming. *'Which one of you took our money?'*

One customer – a retired Methodist minister – told Neeta when it had all quietened down and her own ears had stopped ringing that there had been someone else in the queue right behind one of the two boyos. (They had their phones out the whole time they were queueing. One of them he thought was watching a film.) Young lad, was his impression, arm threaded through the open visor of a motorcycle helmet, though he didn't pay him too much attention. The place was busier than it had been in years – like the bad old good old days. He noticed the bag more, on the ground at the young lad's feet. He remembered thinking 'two Lidl bags', because that was what the boyo in front had too, reaching down every so often without taking his eyes from his phone to drag it forward by the straps another few inches. The minister was turned talking to the woman behind him – a former member of his flock, first day out since she had her hip done – so he didn't see your man with the helmet go. Fed up waiting was all he thought; if there hadn't been someone to talk to he would have been pretty fed up himself, last week or not. Anyway, the young lad went, him and his helmet and his Lidl bag. Or the other boyo's Lidl bag, as it now seemed. Hell slap it up him and all his mates (God forgive him for saying it).

When the other two – the ones who arrived in the car – had gone too, Neeta said, the whole place erupted in laughter. Sounded like the customers had been hanging on to it for years, decades even.

The local news that night made no mention of a theft, though the disturbance on the road was noted. Police, said the newsreader, preparing to slide the page to one side (sports results next), and giving the word an end-in-itself rather than means-to-an-end quality, were 'investigating'. The news the following morning was of a pipe bomb 'believed to be in connection with yesterday's disturbance in east Belfast' thrown at a house in a nearby housing estate – it failed to explode – and, the morning following that, of a 'crude improvised device', which did go off overnight, on the windowsill of another house, children aged eight and eleven months asleep upstairs.

It seemed the men from the Post Office were pointing the finger of blame for the loss of the-money-that-wasn't at one of their own pals, or ex-pals, with whom they had as often been at war, as they liked to say, as they had with, as they liked to say even more, enemy combatants.

That initial cheer felt by the people queuing in the Post Office (and by Herbie, if he was being honest) began to feel a little misplaced.

How often had joy turned like that to ashes in the mouth? How often had little spats spread and consumed large parts of the city until they slowed its traffic to the pace of the funeral processions they created? He began to fear that this one would not end until there were men in white shirts and black ties walking three abreast, carrying wreaths with the initials of one organisation or another.

All this he communicated to Beth, in his daily phone conversations, listening in her responses for any indication that some of the details were not entirely news to her.

She gave none.

She did tell him, in the course of the call on her third day back, that two young men had been stabbed to death in her part of South London in the less than seventy-two hours she had been there. Another four men and an eight-year-old girl had been shot and wounded outside a house where there was a party going on.

Too early to say yet what effect that would have long term on tourist numbers in the area.

He hung up, still not able to tell one way or the other.

There were a couple more incidents: a shotgun blast directed at a car parked outside a social club (missed), an oil tank set alight.

And then out of the blue there was a press conference.

Of slightly greater moment to the wider world than the closure of a sub-post office on a B road between Belfast and County Down, and matters consequent on it, was the twentieth anniversary of the signing of the Good Friday Agreement, which fell on the Tuesday following.

(Would the Agreement at Twenty have recognised itself still in the new-dawn photographs from the time, or have looked at the assembly that didn't assemble, the power-sharing executive that executed no power, and thought that its identity too had somewhere along the way been stolen?)

Rooms in the new hotels had been steadily filling up with journalists and television news crews and the advance parties of minders and spinners for politicians who had spent the past two decades growing into wax models of their former selves.

It was too good an opportunity to miss.

The day before the main event, loyalist paramilitary representatives appeared in time-honoured paramilitary representative fashion, at a long table draped in blue cloth, flanked by leaders of the various Protestant Churches, whose shirts beneath the dog collars were always more colourful than you remembered. One of the churchmen read out a statement saying that no one had an eraser for the past, before he addressed the future, by way of the present moment, calling for an end, with immediate effect, to all forms of criminal activity by members of the organisations the other men at the table (who nodded throughout) represented. He – they – the statement – went further. Anyone engaging in such activity at the expense of their own community was no more and no less than an affront to the true principles of loyalism.

A declaration of transformation they called it.

Herbie had lost count of the number of times paramilitary representatives or the clergymen who flanked them had come out with statements like that – rejection, repudiation, even remorse. Too many for him – or anyone else he spoke to in the course of that particular Monday – to set any great store by this latest… iteration. If it had the effect of calling a halt to the mayhem that the butterfly wing of Paul's revenge had unleashed, though, that would at least be something.

Wouldn't it?

★

He didn't even attempt the Records Office the day of the anniversary. Too much disruption. Bill Clinton was in town: an actual presidential motorcade on top of the city's daily rush-hour tribute act! Belfast, for all the recent expansion, the north- and eastward spread, was still not big enough to accommodate so much fame in one go.

(The November day, several years before, that MTV first descended with its cavalcade of stars, the traffic was worse than the Bomb Scare Fridays of old when five tactically abandoned cars could induce gridlock and grant everyone a not altogether unwelcome early end to the working week.)

It figured, even so, that with all this out-of-jointness he would despite his ongoing precautions and diversions finally bump into Louise, that same afternoon, as she came out of the insurance broker's on the city side of the building that was no longer the Post Office and not yet Clean. She looked as though whatever she had been doing since last he saw her agreed with her very well.

'What's the matter,' she said after a moment, 'you boycotting us or something?'

'Just having to watch my pennies a bit more these days.'

'You know, we price match with all our major competitors,' she said, blinking robotically. He replied in the same register:

'I will be sure to bear that in mind when I am next in need of provisions.'

'How's…' she floundered.

He thought for a split second it was Tanya she was reaching

for, but she would have had no way of knowing anything of her illness. 'Beth?'

'Beth! That's awful of me,' she grimaced, 'mental blank.'

'She went back to England at the beginning of last week.'

'And are you…?'

'Relishing the peace and quiet? Not so much.'

'You wouldn't think of moving to be closer to her?'

'I don't know. I might.'

They walked a way together, an inch-wide force field between their upper arms. She stopped eventually, looked him straight in the face. 'I meant what I said before, I really enjoyed the time we had together, you know.'

'I do.'

'Good.'

'Excuse me.' A man with a white stick wanted past. They both took a step back. 'Thank you.' A few yards further on he turned. 'You were saying, "I do,"' he said in Louise's direction, 'and you,' he said in Herbie's, 'were saying "Good."' He waved above his head. 'Just in case I interrupted anything important.'

'Do you think it would disappoint him if we told him that was everything I had to say?' Louise said.

He watched his feet eat up another half minute's worth of footpath, in step with hers, then out, then in again.

'This is you here, isn't it?'

They had arrived almost without his realising at the corner of his street. Bin day. Dark-grey wheelie bins left every which way on the footpaths by council workers under ever greater pressure to empty more and faster. She stroked his cheek in parting, open palm, then back of the hand. It was all he could do to stop from holding it there. 'Call in and say hello some time. Brian misses you too. Apparently you are his best audience.' He wondered if people had actually *died*. He wondered too, as he carried on down the street alone, if he might move across the water right enough. 'Give it five years,' he said under his breath, 'and if doesn't work out…'

Yeah, right.

He had, what, four, five lots of five left – *hands* – six at an absolute stretch, after which dependency beckoned, or (you would like to think some residual sense of self-respect would kick in) the exit door.

'Excuse me… Herbie.'

He had nearly reached his front gate. The woman across the road – her, Audrey Bannon – was standing at her gate, next to her bin. He tried to think if he had ever heard her voice before. He had expected it to sound thinner somehow, from being so long constrained. There was a trace of somewhere else in it. Donegal maybe.

'You wouldn't have such a thing as a hammer, would you, or a brick?' A faint smile at the absurdity of it. 'I've gone and locked myself out.'

He walked out into the road towards her. 'Is there nothing else you can do? No one you could phone?' he said and straight away knew there wasn't. 'Wait here, I'll see what I can find. Unless, do you want to come over?' Again, he knew, she didn't. 'Wait here.'

The toolbox was in the second place he tried, underneath the stairs, underneath a pile of other crap. He imagined as he opened it the tools blinking. The claw hammer lay aslant in the bottom tray, the thing around which all else had always had to fit. He lifted it and its accumulated history, pictures hung, climbing frames built and in the fullness of time dismantled, and brought it outside.

'Do you need a hand doing this?'

She took the hammer from him. 'Not unless you want to hold the bin for me.'

She dragged the bin up the alley, Herbie following behind, and parked it a couple of feet to the side of the back gate, where, as she pointed out with the hammer's handle, there was a gap in the broken bottles that someone resident there in less enlightened or litigious times had cemented on to the uppermost bricks in the wall for the deterrence of burglars and ne'er-do-wells.

'Don't ask me why, but I stood one day on a stepladder after I moved in and tried to chisel out as much of that as I could.'

She put a hand on his shoulder for leverage as she hoisted herself up on to the bin, hammer in her other hand, and – a quick look down the other side – leg up (he glanced away) and over the wall.

The scene switched then from television to radio drama. A grunt as she hit the ground. Foley artist footsteps (cabbage was it they used?) receding, a rustle of clothing (that was the backswing), a cra—*whoops* (her word) – the glass resisted... He was about to shout, 'Maybe aim further in from the frame,' when she caught it an almighty wallop and the glass shattered, carried on tinkling for a few seconds longer as she cleared a space large enough for her to – climb through? No, he heard, in between the sounds of her straining, a key being extracted – 'Got it!' she said – from a lock. She opened the door from the outside then – Foley artist footsteps approaching (order another cabbage!) – came down the yard and – picture restored! – opened the gate for him.

A stand of sunflowers painted on the nearside yard wall against a background of sky blue, a washing line with a single Marigold hanging from it by a pale green peg, glass all around the back step and what could be seen of the kitchen floor, twice as much you would have thought as was needed to fill the frame it had just come out of.

'That,' she said, 'is why they always tell you not to leave the key in your back door.' She gave him back the hammer, warm handle first. 'I feel I ought at least to offer you coffee.'

'I think maybe you have other things you need to be getting on with.'

A glance behind her, a nod, rueful. 'Some other time,' she said and managed to make it sound like it belonged in the world of plausible future events.

He took a couple of steps down the alley, checked back. 'You can borrow the hammer if it ever happens again, or you can leave a spare key with –' he swerved away from 'me' without noticeable hesitation – 'any one of us on the street if you want. We all do it.'

'I'll think about that,' she said and stepped back into the

yard. He heard the bolt slide home. The crunch of her feet through the glass.

Peadar and Norrie were coming down the street at speed as he emerged from the alley. 'Was that glass I heard smashing there now?' Peadar asked. 'It sounded like glass.' Norrie barked, four sharp barks: it did in-deed.

'It was, but it's nothing to worry about.'

Nothing to worry about? Smashing glass? Peadar drew his head back sceptically. 'If you say so…' He stood for a moment, a man robbed of a mission, but only for a moment. 'Come on, Norrie.'

The dog, which had been fixing to sit, got up – more scrabble than spring (more often the former than the latter of late?) – and loped after him.

Herbie double-checked that his own bin had been emptied then dragged it back closer to the gate. Emmet would be by shortly in his van of many gadgets (a tank of water and a hose, he had started with; now he was driving the Batmobile), cleaning those bins on his list, setting those that weren't, as a matter of common courtesy and wheelie bin aesthetics, straight.

He stopped just inside the front door and was surprised to see a man not old looking out of the hall mirror at him, hair more grey than fair, sure, but *hair*, cheeks ruddied by the wind and the recent flurry of activity, and suddenly the game stretched out again before him, and six or five or even four hands seemed to hold out the possibility – probability – of at least one more change of fortune.

He still did not know how to make sense of any of it, he wasn't sure that he would ever know.

But, so what?

Fill my glass, deal me in, I'm not thinking of folding yet.

He shut the door.

About the author

GLENN PATTERSON was born, and lives, in Belfast.
He has written a number of acclaimed novels including *Fat
Land*, *The International*, *The Mill for Grinding Old People Young*
and *Gull*, and he co-wrote the screenplay of the film
Good Vibrations, based on the Belfast music scene
of the 1970s. He is the Director of the Seamus Heaney
Centre at Queen's University Belfast.